# Misfortunes Of Mister Knack
## by Mike Gutowski

# Misfortunes Of Mister Knack by Mike Gutowski

Mike Gutowski

Misfortunes Of Mister Knack



Cover artwork created by Grace Gutowski

Printed in the United States of America

ISBN: 978-1-7333895-4-9

eBook ISBN: 978-1-7333895-5-6

1. Dark Fantasy. 2. Dystopian Fiction.

First Edition

------

---

Here Begins The Story

The ignorance of innocence served nobly as a much less painful means of existence, especially since the dinner plate full of truths portended an unmerciful bellyache. He had finally arrived. A mess he portrayed, when first viewed, as the arrival occurred after much clang and clash of metal and glass. Sirens blared, sounds which easily could have become confused as trumpet blares, or if in a bleary state, hard fingertip nails strafed across an old washboard. No matter, indeed. Another lost soul had arrived, and perhaps just in the proper time of need.

The cricket chirps created a happiness symphony he had long ago forsaken. Such sounds only emanated true, then echoed into the darkness of night, at a more than appropriate time to raise the cloak of loneliness. Their sound rituals catered a harmony path in the mind of those creatures who appreciated the vibrational balance. It coaxed him into moments of serenity. He allowed the cricket emanations to dominate his ears until they massaged his hearing enough to drown out all other sounds identifiable around and about his environment. A rare peaceful presence remained.

He pleased himself in the quaint delight of such a discovery of human calm resonance. Gradually absolved became all musculature support needs throughout his body, starting at the toes, then along his ankles, shins fore and aft, the spot behind his knees, thighs and hamstrings, gluteus pillows, abdomen and around to lower back, and other musculature needy paths. His eyelids grew heavy. Cricket wisdom trickled wicked into his whined and winded mind. Imagination woes won't become escaped by closed eyes action. Such action bade want to grow in strength.

He returned to the parlor, in measured steps, watched as each foot movement clicked onto the cement path, then mushed out soft taps along the red carpet inside the arched doorway. When a loved one passed on, a void opened in the soul and spirit of those aggrieved by the circumstance. Many memories flooded the mind, eventually narrowed into particularly relevant moments of past interactions and various impressions and extant lore heard from those close to the deceased. The funeral rituals helped family and close friends to grip upon recounts of past common events, sandwiched in between loaves of grief over loss of time with the deceased in present and future.

Remorse over words not judiciously expressed, or words too harshly expressed or iterated in an unfortunate and inappropriate manner persisted none the less. He had lost his religion a long time ago. Still, the grief persisted as a sign the cure for all human ills did not simply rest in ritual or rote ruminations of ancient words. No one escapes the dirt nap. Still, "Funerals are pretty compared to death," Blanche's voice echoed in his mind as a life quote he remembered from a play authored by a brilliant playwriter. A streetcar named Desire stopped for everyone, somewhere along the line, and could become boarded for the proper fee exchange, but mind the gap. Every step loomed as a harbinger of trips. Up, down, farther away, closer together horizons bade.

No more beneficent goodness could become bestowed, and no more sins could soon become inflicted. For some human creatures, love lived more than just as a secondhand emotion. Love could bring them back from the painful brinks of despair. Of course, new painful brinks loomed, as challenges to hurdle, as means to earn and maintain such a cherished find of commitment in kind for another creature lost between the folds of lonely existence. It was rather quiet inside this place. The cricket chirps had become replaced by soft and solemn tune tones emanated from speaker phones mounted in the ceiling corners. The evening's haunts in sounds of voiced wants and nasal taunts effortlessly competed for further attentions.

There's some food downstairs the air revealed, and some comfortable cushioned chairs of high-backed prominence, and cups of happy sipping liquids cold and warm of juices, coffee, cocoa. An odd thought of the post edible processes engulfed him. The arseholes of the mind had been readied for a tense extrication of all nonsense memory threads connected to the deceased, and further in mental degrees, intertwined among the room guests. This memory rambled as pothole bumps of the right front car tire which had it in for him to pay proper attention to the life task at hand, in both of his hands, the steering wheel movements, until the memory crashed into a cogent moment of more pressing need.

Life rolled over the earth realms like puzzles never completed, as loose pieces, and as unused remainders laid about unconnected forevermore. These common social moments resided in memories for a bit until the realities of more prescient exigencies required a need to store them away in an attic of old mind haunts, stored and no longer recalled. Those relatives, friends, coquettes, and acquaintances of related memories would also reach last breaths and move on. Like seeds of grass, they would grow and green in appropriate seasonal rhythms, then shrink browned, enter stasis, reside crumpled or half buried in the grasping soils, then resurrect again as markers of personage passages.

Marcello's "Oboe Concerto In C Minor/Adagio" begged for his listening attention, but he still remained for his duties to plow along the roadway in search of another sale in service to daunting winds and kicked over mettled pales of the ply his noble trade demanded. It was a bedtime sound anyway. He must remember it for slumber time which remained still so off in the distance and so far away in time as it might be. It checked upon his mind to the point he had to vehemently object, yet still he considered a break of his time to concede such a need. He tried and then strained to beg them off, such thoughts.

Grainger's "Walking Tune" begged interruption, and he thought perhaps for good reason. If he pulled off the road, took a walk, he might stretch the kinks out of temptations to rest in a nap trance. He might miss the sale opportunity if he diddled too long on the sleep path. A plethora of such intuitive and counter-intuitive admonitions and morals reached a point of mental plague. A rousing march tune would do the trick, snap him out of a zombie type of state, yet none would bring themselves forth from behind the sound curtain, although he had heard and enjoyed the vigorous sounds of many previously.

He well learned and then filed as knew, long ago, the purpose of the metal watch granted to all who made it to thirty years upon retirement. An object reminder it was. Served as measure of usage. A compartment of time, such device represented. A piece of it laid frozen in a manufactured circle, to click and tick, and remind his head of the moments used, moments lost, and at the last those moments of regret yet to come. "Alright, alright, I'm getting there," he loudly castigated himself.

The shelf was dry in this moment. Where was Sousa at this event of audible need, he wondered. Instead, Lvov's "Violin Concerto In A Minor/Andante Religioso" squeezed out from the sleep recesses of his mind to attempt a spooning of tart elixir, tempting the pall of a smokey haze and tiny-dotted stare gaze of little hope for escape. Evening tones further continued an assault as Grieg's "Peer Gynt Suite/Solveig's Song" finally completed his mind melt, but he managed to at least come to a stop on the side of the roadway, out of the traffic lanes, before slumber strangled him. Puzzle solved.

His last physical recollection remained the feeling of his hand on the transmission shift lever, and the click sound of the engaged parking gear. His eyelids laid heavy as if a penny had been taped to each one. The wind swish sounds of passing vehicles on the travel part of the roadway attempted to jar him away from the sleep web, but to no avail. He remained frozen of physical movement response, captured by the spider of sleep temptations.

"Find me a yesterday and I'll plan a tomorrow," he often said to himself. Many yesterdays he found in music of times past and present. A cloud, it floated along high and long for his mind to rest inside and sometimes upon, for a better view. The land of "Beyond Reproach" still evaded his destination efforts. Some things in life acted that way. Ran from the grasp like feral cats, until they decided to turn and attempt a bite stinger at a moment least expected, as means to accentuate the deed's purpose. Musk, mesquite, mescal aromas and tastes all about and around until dizzy minds were felled to ground. The bridge to tomorrow remained always hardest to mine and find.

In his much younger days, he had tried use of over-the-counter drugs as energy stimulants, yet they thinned his blood to a degree of an elevated pressure level. He gave them up, and then tried a lesser volatile means of stimulations such as a chew of fruity gum sticks. Thick jaw line muscles resulted. He didn't mind such an effect, but eventually gravitated to the tasty temptations of hot coffee, then cooled coffee in the mid-day hours, then hot coffee again later to fend off the evening's chills. The long avenue of varied sweeteners and liquid enhancements of flavor tickled, or maybe tricked his fancy for years, until he finally tired of them, and took coffee black.

He too had noticed another effect in the form of somewhat violent dreams, of being chased by a phantom demon of some sort, not quite visible in the shadows it wore as a cloak to hide itself. It would reach out to him, towards his back, as he ran hard to escape the grasp of it, but sometimes it caught him and created horrid back spasms that shook him awake, sometimes in odd physical states of chaos amidst bedcovers. Chopin's Nocturnes seemed to somewhat but not always ward away the night demons, which he happened to discover when changing the bed-table side radio knob on a motel room's evening rest stop.

Eventually, he determined to turn and fight, which worked only to the degree he could wrestle in the grasp and tug moments an avenue towards awakening, at which time he struggled against air absent of any form. Perhaps he fought himself, he thought. His dream opponent never revealed itself quite visible, remained a bit fogged in a mysterious darkness. He thought on this issue for some time, in attempt to discover a solution. To fight even to a draw was a win, but he began to realize a waking real bedmate would suffer during these dream state wrestle matches. Sometimes his awake thrusts struck the body of his bed partner of the time. He resolved to sleep by himself only, no matter the social circumstance of an evening's endeavors.

In debate with himself over appropriate counterpoints to his Nocturnes supposition, he noted to see also Mozart's "The Queen Of The Night" as a morning wake up musical elixir. The name belied meaning for him. it seemed more a call to night creatures, almost a breakfast call, or hunting horn beckoning the march to food sources, in however violent a manner that march may proceed for animals and insects and arachnid creatures of the evening and early morning sup rituals, in need of necessary survival sustenance. Note also for a hearty day beginning in the human realm, he was reminded Chopin's Mazurka's could tighten the morning ritual into a taught band of purpose. Of course, after a good sales day, the pre-evening ritual required a Dvorak Slavonic Dance. "No. 7 In C Major Op. 72" worked simply fine for celebratory after thoughts.

In some of these sleep moments, he recalled his childhood. Schumann's, "Scenes From Childhood, Opus 15" helped him to reminisce of more innocent times in a mind not crammed by so many worrisome details of foibles bestowed by human existence, inclusive of the cuts, scrapes, harsh words spewed from angelic voices, lessons learned from unexpected pains of loss, expected uncomfortable tasks and events to perform and attend, and pangs of hoped for fantastical holiday events and toys. Moments and objects often became broken into pieces, too much so for a small and as yet undeveloped mind of maturity experience, so the errors and omissions of these events fled to a storage place in the mind, for to become dredged up much later during the age maturation process. Advanced hindsight cured many of the pre-experienced ills, but not all. Never all. Baggage old lay hidden in the back of a closet where light never dared to shine again. The primary youth fear of boredom only became conquered at an advanced age when the dire condition was welcomed like a lost comic book found again. The morning of day would soon beckon another contribution from him. A band of birds began the chimes.

The darned mosquito finally determined to leave him alone, after many appetizer bites of his left wrist and hand. He swished at it several times, only to find it had returned, dogged him further and further, until he lost sight of it during faded glances, then the sound of it disappeared, and finally the smell of the air about the car interior glided gently away from his smokey nostrils, as if a new wind current had swept it away.

The last road sign he passed, while driving along this unfamiliar sales route, read "Unreal Realty", or so he recalled. He laughed to himself about that sight. He wondered if the owner of the company was named Unreal, or if someone in the neighborhood was playing a joke on vehicle drivers. He felt a brief chuckle sufficed in service to memorialize the moment. The arch of any moment gained support from the tensile strength of sense titillations. Just as there existed no method in madness, there resided no discernable calculation for sadness. Just as the coin of heads on both sides offered no choice, even in the random sphere of possibility, existence could not be chosen or decided by a flip. Wisdom had become a fungible and recycled commodity, or perhaps it always was and always would be, a temporary enlightenment notwithstanding.

The human body can appear, upon exploration, as a waterfall, or otherwise as a deep and dark cave. Only the explorer learns, for better or worse, in the act, and the execution of such endeavors. The human mind, on the other hand, is a work in progress, clouded in mystery, masked by external senses reactions, couched in a ready to strike mode, no different in style and fit than a lesser species predator. The lie in wait, the jump from the gait serves similar purpose. For to eat, drink, and be merry, somewhat measured in the digestion aftermath, itself acts out mysterious.

He abhorred the many entrances upon the mind stage of thoughts, but after many years of attempted adaptation to the process, he remained somewhat a slave to the machinations of mental movements, his own primarily, as a start. The entrance to any place physical or otherwise, foreshadowed what was to come, buried deep in the initial presentation, masked. An equilibrium status required exploration of the highs and lows of the scale, what weighed up or down upon the center point of the axis. Steadfast, flexible in nature and demeanor remained choices tempted a burst by all encounters interior and exterior of the human form. If life weighed hard, the question arose about what remained as the alternatives. To breathe or not to breathe begged as the question, for humans and alike species' biological forms. A beauty queued to pee.

Attitude, aptitude, altitude all took away breathe. One more inhale than one more exhale remained the stout goal, sometimes humble in appearance and gesture, sometimes controversial in application. To his right, just outside the car window, in the distance he spied browned leaves falling from an old oak. Swatted they had been by invisible hands of wind currents. "Don't grieve for that which has fallen from your life," he reminded. "Other seasons of opportunity shall come and go." Sunny days and storms would intervene into the crowds of human condition at their leisure. Sometimes a pleasant rhythm balance could only become maintained upon the splat of a fall. Every day harbored a bevy of human seasons, knocks, and resulting bruises. The invisible hands of viruses reminded him of his purpose. A sniffle, a nose drip tweaked at his soul, and lowered itself carefully upon his hairy upper lip. "Need a razor," he reminded, "and more tissues."

A rhythm intoned from the falling rain. He just noticed it. When each drop alighted in the past the sounds never pinched his specific attention beyond the tap and pat impacts of each drop. Such speculations too often became distractions along his travel path. He had become tired, so the car he pulled over to the side of the road and shifted it into the Park gear, turned off the ignition, and rested a bit.

Necessity bred particular ritual both evil and good. Lack of sales progression loomed as the evil. A rest to refocus and energize served good, given a too-close encounter reminder of an oncoming tractor-trailer, too close because he had nearly dozed driven directly into the path of the tractor's monster beamed grill work. Do, done, next. Do, done, next. Do, done, dead. That last option he hoped to avoid a bit longer if he could.

The only matter at hand seemed choice. To make the choice and live with the consequences lurked around every corner of human moment. His sales route taxed his mind a bit. This mapped part of the State remained less inhabited than most he worked. No one at the sales assignment office wanted work tasks shed upon them in this territory, but specific given reasons remained mysteriously vague. Jokes audibly flew across the desk groups more in the dark humor vein than could comfortably become fathomed immediately, about this territory being the most haunted in the County. Varied apparitions, odd creatures cited as legends in lore, had been sighted in the woods which bordered the long roads.

During his travels, romance languages begged a usage interlude for enablement of cerebral scene description enhancement, but alas, he hadn't taken the time to familiarize specifically his acquaintance to the educational opportunities in such regard. French, Spanish, German, Polish he didn't know. It was only English stuck to his tongue . He dabbled in unofficial efforts of the latter linguistic endeavors, but not towards the point of even marginal competence attainment.

The road surfaces harbored some clues regarding movement viability and necessity; and the impact of prior climate events; and civilian vehicle and otherwise creature paws or claws encounters. Road surfaces deemed worthy of foot pad or man-made vehicle machination transgressions had been constructed in varied bands of concrete, asphalt, and some mere dirt paved. Visions of the road right outside the windshield area and just over the edge of the hood, collapsing under his vehicle, flooded his tired brain. He tried to exorcise his mind of such thought hauntings. The storm seemed to follow his course along the road, but he knew such a circumstance to involve mere coincidence. He had seen such sights previous, and knew them to be unusual in look, but regular in occurrence, once the weather commanded such a path. Perhaps he acted as magnet for precipitation. He attempted to rationalize a reason why, but never a creative enough conclusion presented itself upon the stage. Always the ending, elusive remained, and rested uneasy upon his stage.

A roadside "Olde Antiques" sign presented itself as too tempting to resist. The painted black arrow at the bottom of the signpost showed the way. He swatted away the jagged thought of the sign's word usage redundancy. He pulled the vehicle steering wheel and a somewhat reluctant response to the tug spooked him. He didn't need vehicle mechanical issues squirming around like a sun's ray exposed bloodworm just picked from the dawn's light and dew carpeted soil by mother robin. In his mind this far away from creature comforts location had created enough of troubling agitations. Into the cracked and hole pocked asphalt road to his right he and his vehicle ventured.

The mystery and magic of an antique shop visit in the area stocked his senses. The imagination pleasantly responded to such titillating discovery possibilities, of ancient, mysterious, hole and otherwise intrigues. Still, he was reminded of the hole in his soul, the one unfilled by companionship of any star or stripe stimulation. He spied the little in width yet long in length one story in height shop's façade. Rustic and yellowed exterior wall clapboards stared back at him. Whether the exterior emanated an intrigue of times long ago or served merely as more modern design created as visual tempts, he desired strongly to determine. Such a question posed, by means innocent, to the proprietor may become deemed as ignorant or insulting. He dismissed the thought. On the roof's edge, near the dent marked rain gutter downspout which marked the boarder of the shop's edge, a cardinal chanted in love song enchantment tone.

Smetana's "The Moldau" sounded a calm serenade in his mind, or from an unseen porch speaker of the antique shop. He was unable to determine a sound source point upon immediate introspection, so strong was the magic here, just on the shop's outside, as means of surrender to the visual temptations now laid masterfully before him. He stepped onto the porch yet resisted entry until Smetana's magical and mystical sounds abated. He recalled his want of this orchestration played at his funeral some day during a memorial ceremony. Smetana time begged his attention enough to permit a deep visual inhale of the small window display to the left of the entry door frame. Many object details sparked curiosity. Gems, of varied shapes and depths and forms, some pointed or curvaceous or both, sparkled at him. Multi-colored figurines of beings and creatures created an explicit and imaginative form as they reached towards his soul, stretched down from the interior ceiling, latched upon and from silky strings of mysterious sheen called to him, in languages he could not interpret.

His observation path transformed into a purchase list of purpose as if he had become bewitched. He felt it coming to the forefront of his thoughts as if called by words of incantation, but resistance he tried, in the skeptical and frugal taunts, but he feared the previous ravages of driving time weakened such an effort. He realized a battle would rage within him if he reached for the front doorknob, turned it, and began an entry, but the Smetana sounds ended, and before he knew it, he was standing on the other side of the door, closing it slowly. After a deep breath calm he allowed himself to exhale for to call forth a protective temptation cloak.

Given his age, he had become quite familiar of the intrigues and dangers of a shopping excursion. Better to shop without the wallet or clutch, but sales work prevented such preparation. He could leave the money in the vehicle, but on the chance of mischief lurking in the shadows, no such action guaranteed safety, and even risked a worse result. No money, no vehicle, and lost time of immense proportion pursuing corrective measures of such circumstances.

He calculated needs and wants. Need gloves, want a blue insulator. Need 12 pairs of socks as his feet sweated a good bit during these road trips, and he changed them out two or more times a day. Along the walk from his car to the shop front door, he found himself touched by an uncontrollable wonder.

He had spent more time outside the shop entrance than inside, so he limited his temptations to eye darts back and forth until an unusually obvious ocular trap ensnared his senses. By course, he had to look up and down and all around to filter out need versus interest versus curiosity, and so too the next battle of the moment's event commenced in his soul.

He was left alone for a bit as the lady salesclerk went to the back of the shop where there was stored inventory, to find a pair of gloves, as he didn't like the ones on display. while she searched the rear store inventory area, behind a dark curtain, he looked around. A small area displayed signage of odd thoughts. The one most unusual displayed the words "Yesterday Todayed Tomorrow". He reflected on the meaning despite his irritation at incorrect verbiage. A slight twinkle sparked at the corner of his left eye, so he glanced in that direction. A bluish tint buzzed at his mind amidst shelves of old glass-like objects.

"Oh my. Is it? Could it be?" he wondered as his random gaze had perhaps captured for him a mystical shop treasure. He spied as maybe found the mythical blue insulator he had read about, as he did much reading along these trips, when bedded down, or resting in his car, and learned of the rare blue insulator, he purchased one once, at another part of his journey, but it was a fake painted by someone who tried to cash in on the legendary blue insulator craze. he found one in the shop and prepared to negotiate a price when the clerk returned with some gloves. it was cold out and his car heating system had become finicky with age, sometimes resting along the trip by not heating up the car.

She came back to the counter and said, "I believe I found the perfect gloves for you." He looked at them, enjoyed the worn and wrinkled look of experience about their exterior. He next wondered of the feelings of the insides against his hand skin. a soft caress they engulfed his hands in, as if friendly to his skin touch. a warm, comfortable feeling gurgled up from the belly of his insides. as he enjoyed the feelings smothered softly against the terminal, prehensile part of the upper limb in humans and other primates, consisting of the wrist, metacarpal area, fingers, and thumb. they made him feel even more human, as one in need of protection from the cold and damp air of the thickly wooded environment around him, on the outside of the antique shop. One thought, in the background of his mind, began a lurch forward. Souvenirs were important. Memento's, perhaps one like a blue insulator. It represented, in his mind, as a connection point in time, a bridge of past, present, and future.

After purchase of the items needed, plus the one he didn't, the blue insulator, he walked back to his car. He opened it, greeted by the usual crick emanation from the driver's door hinges. "Forgot the tissues," he lamented. Such laments reminded him of something else to do. He let it ride. Nothing else to do evaded his grasp of the driver's seat edge which awaited careful placement of his behind upon the pressed oval seat landing point, and pressure upon his back craved like wanton hands of fingers long, as comfort. A squirrel at the edge of the parking lot cackled. "I know, little one, I know." His forgetfulness folly had once again double-crossed his noble intentions. "One more day. Let's make it count," he reminded. The squirrel seemed to take notice of his word volume as it peeked in a head movement towards his countenance, then continued a search for the edible sustenance of its nature, acorns, intermittently granted by the parking lot edge mighty oaks' limbs. The begrudging trudging sounds of his shoes upon the parking lot surface dissuaded in him a return to the antique shop door for the tissue loot. The embarrassment of an admission, required of such a return so swiftly to the sales counter, defeated the thought tartly.

There existed three periods in time to allow escape from one to another, when necessary. These moments beamed names of past, present, and future. They terrorized each other, conflicted in their desire and purpose, and proceeded on a course to lay bare the landscape of the human mind in all glory bit and gory detail while inflicted upon the human soul as burden and bearer of all things good, bad, or indifferent in nature. Of course, these mystic good and bad insights hinged upon which side of the life boundary an incident resided. Incidents pocked the lifestyle hierarchy of the human condition, no matter from what station the traveler's journey started.

The tit for tat squabble in the human mind, transferred to other human minds by physical actions, or neglect of necessary or hoped for responses, marked the course of everyday moments. No end existed in such social interactions battles, and in the long course, wars among relations, friends, acquaintances, strangers. Happenstance instigated moments and fate driven intended confrontations sometimes resulted in similar squabble draws. A stare, a voiced dare, a spectral scream telepathed to intended target, and yet no response, particularly in the telepathed method, as an encounter amongst two telepaths bore an infinitesimally small possibility of encounter, but oh how he wondered how such a confrontation would work itself out. Perhaps thought for pre-bedtime meditation, under the covers, while the mind searched for somnambulant tunes and tones, from slumber room windows, or walls, or attic ceilings. "The slumbers of a madman," he recalled a passerby on the street whisper to a sidewalk friend. He wondered if, or how, or when he might enter such state of mind as a madman slumbered. Hopefully never. To step one's shoes upon solid ground, devoid of worry or anxiety, sounded like heaven to his mind. A noble goal even if mysterious in the making. "Much suffering must proceed before such a moment could be achieved," he thought. This particular thought he tucked deep into his psyche, as it seemed to need much interrupted contemplation time. He could recall it and work upon it during mundane moments of task completion, or amidst waiting moments during consumer forays, like grocery shopping, waiting for the bus at a transit stop, or while standing on sore knee joints in the movie theater ticket line. Of course, while standing anytime and anywhere, he was reminded by his conscience to not slump at the shoulders. Bad posture plagued him like a disease. He sometimes longed for the indoor confines of the nearby shopping mall because it played over invisible sound speakers the soothing musical sounds sometimes tweaked out vigorously by Ketelbey's "In A Persian Market".

Life wasn't pretty. He hated reminders of such moments. They, the reminders, forced him to attempt extrication of such moments from his mental presence. The effort many times looked, in his mind, like attempts of a fly to flick and wriggle an escape from the domesticated porch spider's web. A one out of 100 odds attempt the fly wrung from the moment. Vibrations of the web threads commenced, first from the fly perspective escape attempts, and ultimately matched by the vibrations alarms sent to the spider's resting origin. A walking death harbinger or running speed dart projection of the lionized spider limbs commenced. The dark impending death ballet commenced, too.

He couldn't remember the last time he pooped, so he began to wonder if he was still alive. "Probably alive," he thought. Still, he realized he might not be existent in a sufficiently sentient state to understand whether he was still alive, or not. Exploring who was who and what was what became necessary, essential, if he were to begin a travel along the understanding path of his predicament. If the autumn of his death had arrived with preternatural swiftness, he had yet to appreciate the moment's connection. He alighted from his bed, moved towards the bathroom, observed the essential rituals of cloth removal, or at least, adjustment, then sat down on his new throne. He began the usual toilet contemplations of life, love, and each lost in varied methods and manners. A sound he at first couldn't quite identify woke him to the physical moment.

"That was either a dog bark, door knock, or hammer blow."

From where, by what method, and for what means as yet to be determined. He focused his hearing further. The sound emanated upon his ear cavities once more. The sound's approach he tried to identify. Not muffled, so likely not from far away outside. More like an echo, which meant likely a blow to the exterior of the house loomed as cause. The sound intensity increased.

"House blows," he surmised. "Someone's knocking at my front door."

His bowel movement purpose defeated again, he pulled his trousers upward and clothing back towards and along his body into and onto the proper places, then started the creepy walk down the staircase, avoiding the banister in places as his certainty of stability in the wood eluded his inspection confidence. The knocking became louder in sound, almost hostile in tone, as he concluded the front door harbored the sound vibrations. At the landing point, his slippers petted the carpet surface in each step. The carpet was forgiving in this regard.

He approached cautiously the main front door entrance. A sniff of the air about him indicated a humanoid presence. He had yet to meet his neighbors and in fact he didn't realize the existence of any, at this point, except for the forest creatures of ground and air. A meeting of a being he had never encountered, human or otherwise, excited fears inside him but the moment created such anxiety he remained unable to explicitly identify them.

Now at the front door, on the inside, and unable to see through the window at the top portion of the door framework, given his somewhat limited height stature, he waited just a bit more in order to identify the portion of the door from which the sound vibration originated. The knocks sounded more like impatient pounds at this point, and their point of origin was about up to his chin, he deduced from the other side of the door origin vibrations.

"This knocker of the door must be large in size," he thought.

He reminded himself that no adventures started in stasis, that each proceeded upon its own pleasures, so he unlocked the door at the bolt portion and the lock tab, turned the knob to the right, and pulled the door inward a few inches. The rays of sun stung him blind at first, as the house interior light fixtures he had yet to make acquaintance of in their particular fixed locations.

"How may I help you?" He asked in a somewhat plaintiff tone, as the sun's rays invaded his visual spectrum rudely. No response audibly noted. The sun's rays then darted a bit, as if the object blocking them had moved. He noticed a shadow upon the outside surface of the door, from the corner of his right eye, and tensed his body as the shadow seemed non-human and large, like that of a bear, yet he too realized bears don't knock, at least not in the steadied manner of the sounds he previously heard.

"Good luck and happiness to you. Deacon Bone. At your service," a voice delicately emanated in his general direction. So soothing was the sound, he had become compelled, out of curiosity mainly, to pull the door back towards him a bit farther in order to find a better angle to dodge the sun gun ray shots. The aroma of the creature at his doorstep seeped into the main entry way. A tart and somewhat dank aroma emanated, yet not unpleasant, at least to his senses. No ill will to be detected, he opened the door back even further. The pressure of this moment fogged a recollection of his own plans for this day, so a new ritual begged attention, as blessing or curse yet to be determined. Suddenly, a dark pall tumbled in his stomach, not of hunger, but of fear. He failed to bring along with him, as a firmly grasped hand lamented, an object for self-protection besides his own physical body. Still, he didn't sense an invasion imminent.

"I've not requested any services for today. Frankly, I would not know to whom or from where I would request them."

The large being at the door seemed to inhale, to a degree which drew from him his own breath in addition to the air around each. A faint head moment interrupted his thinking. He inhaled back some of the air taken from his own interior of the house atmosphere as caution. He tested his heart for sounds, rubbed his chest on the left side, while chocking the door base with his right foot, although the slipper on that foot resisted the effort somewhat.

"If now is not a good time, we may commiserate sometime in the near future, at your leisure."

He thought about such an invitation. No conditions were placed upon it. No attachments connected by rusty hinges. It seemed agreeable, for now. He knew truth to remain and lurk cosmetically masked in the careful application of deception, so weary he toiled amidst an effort to regurgitate a response acceptable to the ears of his inquisitor. The sound of a theremin, and Chopin's "Nocturne In C-Sharp Minor, Opus Posthumous", entered his mind.

"Certainly," he darted back in response, politely, masking a temptation to reveal his curiosity. He wondered if his tone would be deemed convincing to the door knocker of unknown origin and purpose. The door knocker extended some oral tidbits his way.

"Very well. A gathering happens from time to time at the far end clearing in the woods. One is expected to occur this evening. If on a walk, you encounter us, so much the better. You are welcome."

"I am glad to be welcomed. I look forward to the moment," he responded. The large presence exited the doorstep, so swiftly, the sun beam in all of its raw glory and force reflexively bounced his head down to avoid the curtness of visual sting. He closed the door. Returned the locks to secure position, then turned and leaned his back against the door border. His curiosity had not extended so far yet as to require the satisfaction of gains or losses entangled in such a meeting, or any further potential benefits of knowledge to mark as addendum to this encounter. Still, he wondered who "us" meant, by definition.

Two items troubled him steadily during a post-encounter commiseration. Had he just met a male or female personage, and further, he had forgotten to state his own name to the potential guest. The first point he didn't harbor at for long, as the door knocker may not have been able to determine gender either, given the type of robe, and a bit lengthy in distance hair adorning the visage of the interior side of the door holder. What emotions he should feel, or analyze, eluded him, as a result of his own shallow door greeting method. As always, there remained one other issue of the many he was yet to explore about this encounter. The head of the door knocker seemed awfully large. Was it due to a fluffy thick head of hair? Or something else? A conversation commenced within his self, of mind, as he proceeded in the manner of careful steps towards access to the second floor, and the solemn comfort of the bed mattress and covers.

"People tend to not hear what they don't want to hear."

"Perhaps, everywhere."

"Look at your ears, face, hands, feet. They are not identical on each side of your body."

"Perfection is an anomaly."

"In other words, oddity is the norm."

"Thank you."

"For what, may I ask?"

"Understanding."

"My name is Mister Knack."

Once in the bed and under the covers, he searched for feelings. They remained in him, as thoughts. He further explored for sensations. Although dulled, he still remembered them, yet remembrance outpaced any cognizant spark of sensation. He longed to nap further upon this encounter meaning and purpose specific.

Sometimes splinters reminded of skin, and how it exuded feel. Bogle bugle boggle burgle. There existed a wind in the willows that blew more than calm, but it could not be trusted, nor undone, for the scent belied any hint of solemnity. Perhaps the devil had taken him down, and he remained here until services were required. A loneliness feeling in his bosom rudely taunted at him. If taunts could infect his mind and body, perhaps some physical life remained in him somewhere, even if only in spark forms.

He noticed a movement in the bed sheets. It frightened him. Something small, it was, in size. The movement started near his feet, at about the outer portion of his right leg shin. He slowly moved his leg away from the movement, but the movement followed his leg. The movement continued in earnest, along the side of his thigh but not touching it, just moving as if in a crouch. The bed sheet little hump of movement, about human fist size, continued a trek towards his waist, still not touching any part of his body, but he senses a mission point had been predetermined by this little and still unknown predator.

It brushed against his skin, this little thing, but it was not so small as to seem non-threatening. Some creatures or insects of that size could do some damage, as result of teeth usage or stingers, to his body. He tried to decipher the meaning of what he felt on his skin. He figured he had some cloth garment adorning his body, but perhaps not, for a reason as yet unknown to him.

What does existence become once it's realized what can be seen, or smelled, or heard, or tasted of another object or creature or human essence cannot become physically touched at the risk of loss in the company of such? What if the loss of use of the preceding senses disappeared depending upon the type of encounter? Not just touch, as the object really isn't there, or the object or person tried to speak but you couldn't hear the sound? Or explore other senses such as you can smell them but not see them; or they can touch you, but you can't see them; or you can smell and feel their touches but not see them? He presumed this tiresome feeling prevented a revelation to his front door knocker, Deacon Bone. His mind chided out, "My name is Mister Knack".

The deep splash of a woman's face invaded his moment. "Saved my soul, she did," he thought, yet many times a remembrance of her name remained illusion despite a clear recollection of her face schematic. Unable to connect her name, he became further troubled in spirit. The creature invading this physical presence persisted an encroachment upon his upper right-side limb. "At least I'm on my back, from whence my limbs can rotate forward, for defense purposes," he sighed.

A moving shadow, of insect, traced movement just beyond his window shade. The shadow made two stretches, one to the right and one to the left, then disappeared from his view angle. "Perhaps this movement against my body is a mere muscle spasm, or collection of spasms," he thought.

The average number of days of human earth existence was 28,000 or so, depending on what part of the civilized world the subject resided in or upon. The steps along the way were always measured, from beginning to end. It was just a matter of how steadily.

Steadiness required experience. Experience required trips and falls, and resulting wounds that hopefully would become healed, but not before pain, scabs, and skin surface regeneration. Wounds could become hidden, although not always completely. Badges they were, or menial scourges of burden. He attempted escape of his own episodes. Succeeded. Not always. Never always. One person could evoke many names in perspectives of those others, either human or beast, encountered. Some, the names, he would never know, and some he preferred not to know.

Alone we all existed, in our minds and thoughts derived, and lonely from the perspectives of the others. For we are more than one person. We are the person to ourselves, the person to others. A complete and finished calculation of the elemental process was never accomplished, remained in flux. The goal of the entire purpose summed to an otherwise yet to be determined.

He wondered if Einstein kept hidden in his own thoughts the trumpeted realizations of varied calculations he perceived as too catastrophic for publication. Ostracization meant relegation to servitude of the hermit life. Even the Monty Python entourage might find it difficult to commence a dance in the merry tune sounds of that instrument. He had to ask himself, "Oh boy. Where the frack am I going with this nonsense?" A song commenced, garbled as much, if anything at all, "I like life. Life likes me. Dancing the tune of the hermit crab, and the stinging bee."

He mired in the misery of mistakes made, not so much to his own detriment, but more so towards the detriment of others. He sometimes wanted to vanish as means to avoid errors made that would corrode the present or future of those around him. It took him a while to realize indiscretions, much as a child learns of not merely the effects directed towards him as punishment for mistakes, but later, during maturity periods, what mistakes his poor actions or counsel leveled upon lives of others around him. Proper contrition eluded his grasp.

To remain alone protected him and prevented endangerment of the others. Knowledge accumulation, he thought, could serve as shield. He pursued knowledge like a wronged wasp. Allowed his eyes and mind to sting and stain the pages of many books and newspapers. Seized upon reading moments when time allowed, and even when it did not cede to his addictive wishes, plotted the moments of further syphons of knowledge.

As he aged, books had become his bong and balm. No moment existed where a book was not required close by. At the tip of his fingers, he could unholster the effects of it, turn the front cover, and engulf himself in the world of words. The words sparked his mind in many ways, and in many instances, in directions of no certain destination. A mysterious journey he had undertaken, and that experience was enough to want another second, just another minute, then many hours on end, until sleep clouds beckoned and unleashed a heavy storm upon his eyelids. Even in sleep his thoughts would not rest. They searched as predator eyes search a landscape. Always searched for the next reckoning of inspiration, revelation, tergiversation.

He comprehended the sound of a dog bark. By the tone and frequency, it horned a small dog hole in the wind, for to alert a nearby human, perhaps their own, of a potential threat, or perhaps an over-reaction to perception of such. Another dog barked a somewhat solemnified retort, less frequent and deeper in sound, yet firm in approach. So how was it determined which dog won the debate? Was it the dog who barked the loudest and longest? The dog who prepared measured and infrequent retorts? The dog who barked last. Somewhere in between and amidst his intellectual ramblings, musical sounds of Praetorius, "Terpsichore Dances/ Le Bourrée" began to joyously yet low in sound emanate from fibers of the walls clad in elaborate papers of mystic symbols and mysterious to him flower designs.

From the human perspective, perhaps it was the dog who barked second from last who could claim victory. After all, once one's piece of the bark pie had been served, no more barks were required, unless they were derision barks, intended to illustrate the onward and upward and never-ending and chippy concatenations marked as boring lessons, as if the student listeners could not or never would understand the lessons' meaning. The din receded from perceptions of his ears, mercifully. The decibel level of silence temporarily increased in his mind, until it reached a cataclysm of calm status once again.

He observed his hand, the fingers in particular, as he lay upon his bedding. He raised his arm and thus his hand towards dim light as it infected the interior of this abode he currently called home.

"You're tracing dreams. I'm chasing memories." He forgot who imparted these wards at him, like darts. They struck the mark, not absent pointed pain sparked by derisively taken self-clarifications. He previously bid impalement of this flimsy counsel upon his mind, but it many times escaped and evaded capture. Cretinous goons such counsel lurked hidden, perched high awaiting the perfumed moment of strike. Sometimes dreams that became true evolved into worst nightmares, of his own making. For how can any moment meet encounter possibilities except by acclimation of the target movement towards the inclinations of the host.

Invitation accepted, by chance, choice, or temptation however uncertain the imprint of footfalls was carefully placed; not by compelled gravity pulls, but by random sparks danced to a temptation vibration which pounded forth in him deep, rhythmic, haunting, cobbled together solid of mysterious woe. To break this formed coal piece, or to light it up, and burn a dance to the flame flicks' tempted entrance, penetrated the observer into choice servings' decisions. The words arguing for varied temptations of his deviously random mindsets, chiseled long to discover some meaning, shaped carefully hard, wouldn't let up. Give a human a chance to contemplate and any avenue towards a conclusive destination is possible. Devout dead ends served purposes of the journey. Dead ends served enlightenment goals even in dark spaces.

Unrequited love weighed as laborious loss. Give it away, but receive no returns, until all giving energy drains away. Start as a rock, finish as a pebble. Detritus accumulated as a cobbled path. Darn that dream. Curse it or make it into a pretty picture of anxiety representation, as a reminder. Reminder of what purpose or point lurked in the back of the mind, for later rumination. The latter bucket overflowed. He didn't want to close his eyes again. He didn't want to dream these dreams over and over. He told himself don't go there, but his mind munched the decision as first choice. He told himself we will go there later and satisfied the procrastination quota appetite bites.

A sniff of liquid coffee aroma tempted his rise from the prone position. He didn't recall if he had previously set the pot to make the coffee automatically for a certain time. He didn't recall that he had learned such method as the equipment instructions disappeared during the long journey of organization of objects and mental priorities, somewhere in a cabinet drawer. Since he had recently relocated to his destination, he would now need to search many closed boxes to find a single object of need or otherwise memory jogging. Although the purpose of such jogs always intended to be helpful in the organization project, many times it evolved into random trips of past moments. Past moments became vacation islands in his mind.

Telling of time served not as necessity in this place. Such telling no longer served any purpose. The mechanisms of time measurement remained unreliable anyway. Sometimes they worked in song or tone or click, sometimes not, and no dire moments of recrimination served as punishment from any source foreign directed towards the time moment request or requester. Simply thought, time evolved into irrelevance. A true vacation moment it had achieved. At least the vacation moment when packing and unpacking was involved. Still, the packing and unpacking efforts allowed for infestation into the mind of happy can't wait to do this or that moments. Drudgery deeds served purpose more than a few times as another mysterious elixir in the human life realms.

Anyway, he could judge time by the mannerisms and sound emanations of creatures which inhabited his new neighborhood. He abhorred a thought of arrival when his physical place in this next moment might recede to the point of last breath death. All would eventually cease to radiate as new, and at an exact time point, instantly implement as old. Such threshold he wanted to defend against. To find his way and means to this defense possibility entered his mind journey planner as a priority goal for exploration and future accomplishment. Perhaps the gods in this place of the wood, and the gray sky, and the brown path, and the fog shield, if he could find them, and present himself to them as peach in appearance and demeanor, they would then understand his requests. "Yes. I do remember a fog."

He became remembered of the moments when his knuckles were cracked by a wooden ruler when the teaching order Nuns, in his young schooling days, had commenced a lesson and needed immediate attention from students. He looked at his hands, knuckles side up. They still looked burnt red, then morphed into blueish pain tints. Pains and pleasures easily evoked memories both good and bad. Yellow cautions road signs flittered in his head, tittered around like hard struck ping bong balls bashed into the green wooden tabletop surface. Crack of the paddle surface upon the plastic ball; bash of the ball upon the wood surface; echoed din of the next sound explication, and the moment of each sound mitigated by trajectory of the ball from initial paddle impact to resultant tabletop incursion. A pool stick stabbed against a white round cue ball offered the same sight, touch, and sound obfuscations of feeling.

What could be worse than an old human checking their own body for viability of potential human interactions? Memories of what was versus moments of what is crashed together into a mix of who knows what recipes of potential conclusions. Bathe, shower prep; towel off by dabs and dips. Measure the steps from tub to floor, or make a step nevermore, as the head bangs against a surface too hard for intimate interaction. Mourning doves and crows emanate a cascade of serenade sound for each indelicate moment. Should the promenade proceed by chance or creed, the time for clothing the noble steed arrives, as sight only for lonely or biased eyes, as each linen thread of cord beckons hope for a younger, fitter life restored. Such hope commemorations optional, or as substitute, add High School yearbook ruminations, shredded, and gleaned per taste. Season with noblesse and oblige, the moments proceeded by the sight of sore eyes yet to have awakened to the soaring brightness of olden day's ravages. Serve chilled at your own risk. So, what could be worse? Much. Much could be worse. The blessings of an ability to self-preserve in one's predicament remained reward enough.

It's coming out and prepared for better, worse, or anything cares. Aroma tricks the mind, trips the soul, wrenches the brain nugget. Not as sweet as remembered. Not as sour as tasted. Never exactly the same after preparation. Wait a few minutes. Temperature massages cure every possible variation. A Halloween or Boxing Day of memory corrected. Hindsight's a kill shot yet killed nothing but hope. Get over it or die under it. Either method served the same master or mistress.

Acceptance of thoughts and the very soul essence attached to such emanations, like acceptance of another's attentions, was solely decided by the cogent receptors of each entity engagement encountered. Some participants, whether subjects of accidental or intentional encounters, feigned reception. Some craved it. Some collected the moments as mere souvenirs. Some tossed them away as yesterday's garbage. Some were oblivious to the whims and wares of the many and varied machinations of the entire process. He often wondered what it all meant. He wished for some control over the varied degrees and digressions of it all, especially in the minutiae of real comprehension. Real comprehension many times only existed on the dust particles floating about a habitat, like fairies light in appearance and countenance, and sometimes comprehension wafted amidst the shrill like goblins of soul sucked impudence. Either way posed a death threat amidst the many measures of sentient cohabitation among the other humans and humanoids of any existence world, to and for all creatures, down to the very viruses of every plain globally extant at any given moment. Not perfect in dance steps these moments lived, but necessary in day-to-day travels and transgressive actions. Dash, dart tamely, imbibe, masticate solemnly, rest, toot odors. Daily digressions and impressions masked as real moments a defense against pin-pricked derisions, whether such actions measured as warranted or otherwise. Reason reigned not and existed whole as the exception to not.

Sometimes his greatest restraint efforts had to be preserved for the prevention of thinking out loud. One's truth, however perceived, poked as sharp dagger, and such learned truth must remain sheathed until the last moment of defense had become required. For one's truth may not have been another's coalesced experience of thought, a precious jewel moment it became, when two souls happened upon each other and discovered a similar perceived truth existed amidst their mutual consciences. But for those who happened upon a path of love, it was the moments of intersections that led to digressions of mutually accepted conclusions of reason. In those moments, the exploration of differences became intoxicating, and each taste, aroma, texture of such intellectual touches begged either for further human closeness, or the step back towards abject alienation, as the extremes parameters presented themselves to their respective senses. If they could balance together on such tightrope moments, more time than not, a slim chance still presented itself for further relationship exploration.

For example, his sight touched her skin. He melted inside. Then from the lips of her face, and the tongue concatenations of tissue, word sounds poked his belly hard, then quickly ascended and smashed into his skull, after penetration through the skin and protective tissues, until he became nearly blinded of sight. Repeated whips of her voice chains ripped at his mind, until it could no longer function sentient. When her tirade, from his audible human perspective, had ceased, then his vision again gained ground for perceptive moment and he noticed her lip edges had curled up towards north, at her cheekbones. The words she uttered paralyzed him in a negative manner, yet she found some measure of pleasure for herself in the utterance of her own voice vibrations. For him it served as sensual attack. For her, as pleasurable cuddling. The relationship was over in his mind. Now to figure out a way to conclude all physical entanglements previous threaded into the relationship. He wished to retreat, whole cloth intact, but the measure of his retreat must become weighed in the poundage of gains and losses, marked by cunning and unsubtle movements. He measured the need for words in the moment after her smile, then declined a response, but no response served as response for her, and to that effect he belatedly realized he would suffer doom to her future remonstrations. A fate he in no purpose relished, nor wanted, nor needed. The no's overshadowed the yes's in his mind as to relationship continuance and expansion. The only question for him became how to begin retreat.

Humans touched their world through senses of sight, sound, smell, taste, and other manners available to them. Part of learning, growing, existing involved honing the senses' ability to identify what senses adequately captured a real moment of revelation; of wisdom; of counsel necessary for growth, or stabilization, or harmony. All creatures and objects sensed their immediate world in mystical, spiritual, and physical ways. The senses of each allowed for interpretation of environment and those objects and beings extant therein, and perhaps even thereout. To think of someone or something was to be there, in company and concert of existence. His philosophical ramblings rolled and tumbled and banged against existence in near endless cycles he found difficult and sometimes unable to control.

## The Night Maiden

Miska Moonshaw was perhaps the most adept in development and usage of these traits. As a witch, she learned the arts of sensory manipulation, because in order to control an environment, the only way to command it was to master the sensory machinations encountered. As an added advantage, her age upon the earth ground allowed for greater mastery allowed towards any competitors. He recalled he had met her by chance, or fortune, and somewhere deep inside him a bell-star became awakened. The mystics of the encounter entranced him, and the memory of it flashed so strong he sometimes needed to force himself to forget it, but the moments crashed back into his psyche and demanded attention from time to time. He couldn't even quite recall the first introductory moments, except in a bit of a haze or light gray fog of mind, or was it environment, or a sidewalk encounter, or café mutual shoulder bump of accidental table aisle crossing.

"I believe we have more in common than you realize, or recall," Miska Moonshaw parried first in conversational tone.

"We've never met," Chrysostomus Knack responded, then inquired, "Are you certain?"

"Of our many lives, I would remember," she answered.

They mutually spied an open diner table, seated themselves about the roundness of it, and continued the word parry, each in pleasurable and civil tone variations.

"Of my one life, I fail to recall," he said.

"Would you like relish with that ambiguous roll?" she lightly audible thrusted forward to further tickle his mind cells.

"Alone we are, as I had wished for some time, given our discord of past moments," he returned in some jest, as means to continue the pretend he imagined the oral field demanded.

"Can we end this now?" she requested, as means to call truce, and recollect in demeanor modest.

"Why are you here? People don't usually meet unannounced unless one or the other or both have needs of such an encounter," he continued.

"Perhaps it is fate," she posited for fruitful consideration.

"Perhaps. Fate is a matchmaker, at times," he said.

"Neither of us were perfect persons," she offered.

"Perhaps, in this moment, we can change that circumstance," He said. He looked at her face closely, carefully. Such a beauty of expression he had encountered before, only once. That moment lasted for a few decades, until the perfection of the beauty faded, not in facade, but in spirit.

"Then you do remember me," she voiced in a pleased tone.

"I remember someone like you, in appearance. "In tone of many aspects," he conceded.

"Then our table is set," she said.

"What is it you are serving, in needs?" he continued.

"We are only at the dawn stage of this conversation, yet you seem to want the meal's dusk sooner to arrive," she said.

"Such a waste of day is still a waste, and waste is my enemy," he said.

"Then wait for your pleasure, as if you waited for it all of your life, and never truly appreciated the moment of taste when it arrived," she offered as consideration.

"Is this conversation dashed and dabbed of spell incantations?" he responded, before he could hold his tongue, and merely think such words as an aside of scorn.

"You really need to learn how to mask some of your thoughts. Yes, incantations. No lies to spout or masks to hide behind in veils oral or physical," she advised.

"This entire place of eatery abode and surroundings betrays your words, and thoughts, and very presence," he poked.

"On with the ride, then," she darted back.

"Perhaps a betrayal it was, in moment, I revealed?" he voiced along a low road path.

"If a different scenery is required for serenity secure, just use imagination of your own choosing. Your questions are my answers," she suggested.

Irritated he became, in the realization he was hopelessly behind her in witty accumulated points, yet time with one other sentient being, almost no matter which one, brought meaning and purpose. Still, unresolved in his mind remained where each danced unsteady, out of balance. He wanted balance, craved it, no matter the circumstance.

"I will listen more attentive. I apologize," he offered as concession.

He realized they were sitting, across from each other, at a dining room table, yet he didn't recall inviting her further into his intellectual chambers, although he recalled observation of her body as it rested into a seated position. He thought they had reclined in a restaurant setting. Some difficulty he encountered while clearing his mind to better appreciate the physical surroundings. While watching such movements of a woman or man betrayed much of their character, in the means by which they grasped the chair arms or seat with hands and extended arms, raised the chair or slid it, drew it in towards lower body and legs, the angle of the back and resulting arc figure illustrated strength capacity and determination of the upper body. The direction of the face oval up, down, sideways, and to which side helped spell out a balance of mind, body, and spirit. The remainder of the moment, final rest position from top to bottom, monument regal, or somewhat disheveled and in need of tedious adjustments betrayed further insights.

She must have hidden this moment from him, he thought, to keep him out of balance during the conversation journey. His wonder at the hidden nature of these brief events acted as a harsh and bright light flashed upon his mind, intended, he believed, as a means to disable his attention abilities. A sick and deep fear bubbled up in his stomach. What else could she master in the menu of deceits to disable his means of comprehension, and measures of defense and counterattack. Her perfumed aroma may have started as the source, and now he was completely enveloped in the snare.

"Your dancing is a bit rusty," she offered.

"What?" he asked, surprised at her observation. He looked down, noticed they were physically gliding ever so slightly above the floor tiles, or so he thought, as he could not detect the musculature movements in the legs, or the touch sensations of his shoes against any floor surface. He tried not to feel tense, lest he reveal his emotional discomfort, but she noticed, of course she noticed. He glanced around his body, using his eyes only, for head movements would further reveal his discomfort. But she noticed.

"As compared to what?" he inquired.

"Not what, but when, is the question," she responded.

He tried to regain control of himself emotionally. Her essence, scent driven, and now her physical touch transferred to his own physical natures, intertwined, particularly in the areas of chest, arms, hands offered; comforts he had allowed to slip away from his list of comforts, and he enjoyed it, these experience moments, despite his want to reject the encounter in its entirety, except for the conversation parries.

A conversation is a unique human experience, particularly when it is personal, in a special place, between merely two parties. The experience of each is a special event, of many moments ignited by words or phrases which sometimes spark emotions of anger, regret, pangs of nipping voice bites of the mind, tears of spirit in bits or chunks, but sometimes ignites as revelations shouted from mountain tops. A proper balance of tone, enhanced by glances, direct looks, stares into the eyes of each participant, usually an enhancer of the sparks ignited by the words, furthers the deeds of past, present, or future laid carefully or accidentally into the mind till of the participants. Contemplation time of the word effects extends from the original orations, offers opportunity for analysis.

Immediate and accurate interpretations are sometimes futile, especially if the main distractor is an emotional attachment previously strung around the participants. Parent and child, parent and parent, child and child, boss and underling, underling and underling, authority and authority, authority and obedient, obedient and obedient, friend and friend, friend and enemy, enemy and enemy, acquaintance new among any of the prior named parties creates a theater of possible interactions and portrayals thereafter. He quickly found himself wavering inside and outside of each of the aforementioned categories during this encounter time frame, until desperately he wanted to move into the moment of truth event. He realized he could refuse to listen and dismiss her, or he believed he could do so.

To find the strength and to exert the effort scampered from his mind frequently during the encounter. The proper words, solid spoken, clear, convincing, he attempted of capture. Eventually, he readied himself to die in her arms, so overwhelming became her presence let alone words. The exception to his event conclusion remained whether a revelation future existed as chance. He knew; however, such a possibility became irrelevant if the torture of emotional sense of self evolved as too burdensome upon his mind and spirit. Not just his mind at stake, and not just his spirit to lose, but both, at the same time, or perhaps each to erode gradually, like the metal strong of a building beam in stages of rust development. He resisted a surrender to a crush of all structures about his own being which he had spent much time and effort to build.

His mere presence in this place, the place she also occupied, somewhere exactly unknown to him as yet, confused him, and that circumstance remained the mystery of searing stings.

"Get on with it already," he thought. "What does she want?"

"I want this place. And you out of it," she responded.

His imagination swiftly transferred in space and time from these moments of their first encounter, to the many years hence, on the cusp of their last encounter. He was certain she didn't hear his thoughts. How could she verbally respond so to his physical insecurities, he wondered, and a bit feared.

"This place?" he asked, a bit bewildered.

"Yes," she said in a voice that seemed to fade in tone.

"Exactly what do you mean?" He let go of her, turned his back, and walked away a few steps to regain composure of his voice tone. When he turned back towards her, no one was there. Relieved, he determined to retire for the evening. He wanted to look around the house to find her. Wanted to open the front door and look outside, or just look out the front window, but he resisted. To look further at her, to smell her essence would strengthen the feelings and thoughts which she had just ignited in him and used to invade his mind. Further, he was physically exhausted. He would lay down, sleep on it, and hope a dream state would reveal further connections he could sew into a sentient and usual cloth form. Souls rented sometimes begged for such repairs.

Her aroma persisted upon his clothes, so he removed them, yet it still persisted upon his body, so he showered and returned to the bed. It persisted in his mind, still. He blotted out all thoughts, fell into a haze of near sleep. The voices he heard, but whether of his tone or hers, the words intertwined in meaning and sound, until orator identity lay irrelevant in his mind.

"At some point we have to accept who we are."

"At what point?"

No nods exchanged between them. No agreement reached or point conceded.

"We don't, have to accept who we are."

A spark lit the conversation kindling, just in time for the full flame to acquire true red-light potential.

"You really want to go there, to that location where all is dark and hidden in shadow and queer sounds unable to become attached to any known audible ignition trajectory start, or state, or moment."

"Why not? Why leave it an open question? After all, the answer won't be the same for those who find the wisdom to ask the question."

"Asking the question isn't wisdom personified. It is ignorance inflamed."

"Even if the wisdom switch is tripped, from whatever cause or course, no question should become feared to answer. No cowering of the soul is acceptable in such an intellectual predicament. To avoid understanding is to grab ignorance around the neck and choke it out. I can hear the pleading."

"Right. Please, please keep me blind, deaf, and dumb. The world couldn't handle my feeble attempt at understanding. Has no time for it."

"A stampede of ignorance it would become, stoked by media wizards. A casting of dark spells, iterated loud and long and rank of vowel stale and consonant twisted."

"Oh my, yes, I see your point, or rather, hear it, then see it, then smell it."

"Rude you are in jargon drool."

"We each have taken liberties."

"Yes, to such truth I can acknowledge and too, acquiesce," he thought of saying, to be polite, but temptation angers interceded which led to a blurt uncommon. "The question always remains whether respect is deserved, rather than required." He awaited her response. A silence battered hard into his brain. Time to drift on and into another sub-topic of relevance. His parry thrusted further.

"Regarding relationships. All of those memories of us existed only in a few places, but primarily here and there, in the main," he said, then pointed to his forehead, and alternatively to hers. A somewhat romantic thrust he concluded, as a fine achievement. Closed eyes, he did, as sweet surrender to her silence. He opened his eyes, unable to bear the unending noise solitude. The pounding silence upon his temples caused more self-induced noise shields to raise ready a crouch from behind. His knees failed to cooperate in the crouch. The shield pounded to the floor on edge. It became his temporary crutch upon conclusion of the battle.

Love action and meaning had bored a deep hole into his soul. When continuation of such pursuits became unfavorable, the trip left an un-traversable cavern never again to become filled. "Little devils rest in the revelations of silence, crouched, readied to pounce as syllables mispro-nounced or annunciated," he massaged into his brain thoughts. He had come to realize she had plucked a lost soul, at the roots, from the raw and untilled garden of humanity, replanted it, and out of the newer soil sprang him.

Recounted moments descended from the horizon hilltop, as they did and would more often in these latter times of his life and career. "Either day in break or evening under cloak had commenced," he pondered, too often now. In the scheme of his life events, such moments carried lesser and lesser importance. A lighter mental burden, yes, as old minutes added up complicated, readily crumpled like paper into crinkled little balls, and became replaced by a more taxing purpose revision, weighted against new minutes.

New minutes had begun to take more weight endurance, given the precious existence continuance scarcity. Mister Death could see him, from a distance not so great as years before. Those year paths had been trodden worn. No dead end could he yet see. A sigh of relief massaged his brain cells. The ceiling fan that spun regularly inside his head changed between degrees of obvious in sound, then towards somewhat obscure at other times. He often wondered if a humidity index existed in his brain that controlled the whir vomers.

He looked around the room. No one could he see or visualize or hear echo of voice from. He could have sworn a conversation had become trig-gered by a female voiced presence somewhere in the room. He thought it might be a guest to whom he had not yet been introduced. He seemed to have lost himself. At least, that was the best explanation he could produce to explain his current predicament. He had made visits to this place a few times previous, as his business travels took him past the sign at the side of the road which introduced the property to passersby. The symbol on the sign intrigued him.

Sizing The Journey

Over time he began to investigate the place name, history, and meaning of the sign symbol, but his efforts provided little in information, as if the place never really existed and had become a prank endeavor of some local high schoolers, or perhaps because the sign was meant for taking down by the town overseers, and as many times happens, never got around to it, or perhaps a property in body and life still breathed on the other side of the dense forested boundary between the property heart, and the outer world transgressors or travelers who chanced upon the boundary borders. He made a mental note to himself, "Need to go back there and see what is there, what is happening, is it real."

Something in his gut itched about these thoughts, would not go away for exceptionally long. Every time his travels took him upon this route, the itch grew stronger, almost to the point of unbearable. When stopped in the area at a motel, for work dealings, he would lay upon his bed, during off time, and torture himself with thoughts of a visit to the property, even though he realized there was not time, or perhaps a waste of time awaited as reward for the effort.

When in love, all of the human senses required immediate, almost instant gratification, in a proportion larger than the buffet table permitted in space. The urge fed, endlessly, until it displayed itself as torture of the heart, plague of the soul. When the love feeling splayed bare as uncooked raw meat, unrequited, the emotional horrors began sublimation, yet a big hole remained in the psyche, needed to be refilled as a temporary measure, to move onward along life's path.

Unfortunately, some found the patch merely dug a deeper hole to fill, and the filling became either obsession for food, or exercise, or solemn contemplation moments in high degrees of frequency, which threw body and mind out of sync. A queer dancing act it was, to fall in love, walk the highwire, fall, recover from wounds patched, and walk again. At some point, to not fall in love or become prey to love's temptation remained the safer course. Avoided poor choices, some of which ruined lives personal and peripheral for weeks, months, years, decades. Short stretches of love found, then love lost easily escaped the painful grasp of youth. Random memory punches created a temporary knock down of such escapades emotionally dodged.

Yet, his story eluded the subtle intrigues endemic in love. Love existed merely as chapter, among many verses already consumed and stored in his head. Many yet to read beckoned sometimes soft, sometimes loud, sometimes woefully in need of a good towel wring dry, until his as yet unknown specified time came to an end, when a conclusion to the story was required, despite any unfinished business. He realized also love sometimes died. To surrender into the caverns of some ravenous needs temporarily spared. The other deeds attracted an opportunity for escape, however temporary, to survive another day, not unscathed, never unscathed, but offered, afforded opportunity to better heal.

He realized his thoughts pocked full to the bursting of adjectives, verbs, nouns, and lesser language tidbits had overstocked his mind. He begged them release and given his practice of escape from their sweaty grasp, his release was granted, if not earned. Vigilant of their haunts, he had become, on a regular basis, but he realized some mental rest would do him good prior to their next assaults, which always seemed planned on the other side of the hill. They hunkered down, and he did too. Replanned, rested, planned again, tested in theory, they went along until the point of readied for the next assault and defense, in either direction of command. To capture some clarity of the moment became skill. Practice helped much in the longevity of his life. A ring sound tolled at him.

"Don't give me a reason to answer a phone,." he voiced into the hollow alone of the room's cavernous borders.

Age had caught up to him and leapt upon his hindquarters. Then it clawed upon his back and squirmed towards his neck. Opened a sharp-toothed and salivated jaw from which greedy hunger drips spilled and splashed away. The damp jaw then clamped down. One moment away. Always that one moment away from the final shake which would break his neck. The phone ring sound stopped. He glanced around the room, squinted at the shadowed places, but could not locate the phone origin.

"Give me a reason. A reason to think." He shouted to himself, "give examples!"

What was known leered at him scary. What wasn't known loomed, remained even more so as a jittered fall. He shook the mental eight-ball globe. The white words inside it streaked, meandered, swayed until focus cleared a single word.

Food. He smelled it and wanted it. When younger would find it and eat it. He sniffed in the air an aroma of cooked bacon strips, four or five, gracefully laid out upon a small dish. He spied in his mind a porcelain plate of scrambled eggs, about three he guessed, abutted by a side of hashed brown potatoes. Butter squares and jellied pods in plastic wraps tempted a spread upon two medium brown toasted white bread slices. The aromas greeted each other in a respectful courtesy, then united in a victory clench of hands, gradual communion of bodies, as an aroma dance began movements divine. Now, the smell temporarily quenched until the hunger urge receded to a manageable level. Belly aches avoided, for now.

Ditto for the liquid pleasures. Swam their streams, rivers, and oceans carefully, then drowned in whirlpools unseen too late. Coffee black, tasty sweeteners and enhancement products declined. Juice orange, diced on the spot, awaited the satisfactory pucker of quenched thirst lips.

The world, in the baking process, existed somewhat less than the who you know, and more about who you fornicated with. Of course, fate and forced circumstances beggared, and an audience in all matters human or otherwise along the evolutionary path progressed. And still of course, some of the higher intelligence-based sentients believed there prevailed a balance between each. A social study, conjoined in a biological study, in somewhat of a mating manner, post-dance amidst elemental Dane influences, may yet prove itself as the veil lifter.

"We have no idea."

"Yes. Speculation spices the mix, disguised as essential ingredient."

The interjected moment matter, a Manet effect upon society, in presentation, beamed in curt visions and then spoken in words of vague recognition, buys still as voices his brain projected into his conscience and flew the avian path as lesser views along the horizon, as such matters sometimes gently did. Sunset still prevailed in the artistic perspective, for now.

Currently, the sample size generated by such turgid ruminations seemed yet too small in size and scope. His thoughts seemed dope to him, so he allowed them to interject along this self-enlightenment course. Plus, fate and folly played a mix in the beat, just as voter fraud in the human history of forge and foil, all conjoined amidst congestion and indigestion demons beckoned a say of words or biological spewed dirges, at one time or another, as shined and crafted assignments of noblesse oblige destinies incubated slow and soothing in the governmental oven of pre-poisoned societies. Even in nature, poison dashes to some, becomes member and remembered, as the succubus succulence of all creature status community existences. Just remember to save an empty seat for the future unexpected and unaccounted for guest or more.

An open door begs the walkers of the moor, tempts entry upon the doorstep. Whether to lock them out as means to assess their intentions, or suffer the consequences of an uninvited trespass, remained a question. Trespassers always beg assistance. The guest question, somewhat a guesstion, in such matters sounded out as for who's benefit. Whims gleamed as dangerous means of assessment procedure, in practice. Consumption needs existed to promote function. The process, from beginning to end, bore temptations and hazards burden, and later, perhaps pardon.

Sensory elements all became tempted like a fate whirlpool, before feast, during feast, after feast. To see beauty begged a want to touch it. The rose counseled otherwise, and sharp and pointed stem thorns reminded patience ruled over unbounded instinct. The senses could fool the fool or make the fool. The jester's curt wisdom needed interjection into the mix.

Folly needed to rule, sometimes, as noble guide, yet cultures cut down the beanstalk to redemption many times and places, as if they feared truth and wisdom, and rather preferred darkness and skullduggery. Dim light and dishonesty masked warts of civilizations like sauces and spreads hid molds of growth upon the meal bread. Comfort promised as much a chaos as the busty city street tortured by the malfunctioned traffic signal. Efficiency ruined. Safety breached. Efficacy drowned. Harm attempted a jail break.

The daily purpose mathematical function had become a mind twist and mental curse that would leave a wearied traveler, innocent or not in purpose, weaned of prior conceptions and misconceptions, to equal the remainder as never the same again. Much of life involved making choices, implementing the plan to succeed poorly, and not adequately compensating or stepping back and starting over in a better place to create a better situation. Hindered by poor thinking or planning or the fatal combustible combination of each, resulted in wrong conclusions made during implementation of plan, failure to adjust, makes changes; emotional roadblocks and scars; mental roadblocks; intellectual poor preparation remained readied at the gate, awaiting the starter's pistol shot and subsequent bang to begin, to unleash the taut musculature of chance and effort and zoom. His ears could hear, as musical haunt that leached upon his skin being, the tone taunts of Faure, Whisper of Angels (Pavane). And the moment was good, for the short time it lasted to stem the tide of another pained breath required of existence in the extant world. The shadow of Death's gaze never relented in spirit and cause. It hung around accompanied by broom and Lloyd Ray's dustpan to wipe the mess. His mind counseled him once again of life encountered literary and musical quotes imbedded upon his psyche, then settled in aside two.

"Even in the grave, all is not lost." - Edgar Allan Poe.

"Wish I didn't know now what I didn't know then." - Bob Seger.

He knowingly realized the demons of memories would continue to haunt his mind house. This lifetime cask of associates and acquaintances too had wronged him, his perspective countered in argument. A tit for tat streamed in conscience randomly, perhaps also in the opponent minds. "Not to consider as waste of time," he self-counseled. But regrets and mental flagellations never quit the purpose. These characters perceived he wronged them in his life moments, one way or another, through neglect, violence, ignorance, or mistake. He didn't wrong some of them according to his own recollections. Yet, he surmised they sought to foist an after-life revenge or punishment upon him, or combinations of each, for to convince him to seek penance or retribution during his life. Even from some of them he perceived a revenge bend in path because they were cursed by an inability or debilitation deep which prevented absolution of themselves in such dead restful purpose.

During human social encounters, a smell, or taste, or appearance facial quirk, or word usage tone sometimes down to the very syllable pronounced, or cloth and jewelry dressage methodology could jolt a temporary inability of the observer to see beyond their own mask and costume into the land of mysteries, delights, and temptations of an alternate observer. A psychological truss casted upon their own face, or shield thrusted in front of their own body, as defense against unknown emotion invasions darted from the crowd beings, or guest introductions, or planned meets and greets. He had worn out his welcome on these thoughts, then ran from them until exhaustion grasped a gasping halt of mind.

Of where he stood with himself, the answer eluded him still. Fits of awake. Fits of asleep. Fogged paths of in between stretched out and peaceably served as breach for each time period of his life. Certainty of how long each period lasted concerned him as faithfully as plantar fasciitis. Perhaps his dogged certainty of long ago had now betrayed him in this moment. Betrayed by his own memory as it vomited the horrors of life, from his perspective moments, upon his own chest, to rest there and slowly compress him into one last breath. Or memory it was that washed and waved of a bad cold, tempting the pneumonia to join in the fun of a ravager dance upon his bosom. Restoration to old home earth beckoned. Slow rolling streams of woe infected his thoughts alternately. Every room of the mind harbored a potential lesson, for the willing student, the listener, the practitioner, willing to skin the knees along a stony practice path.

Of course, his life's perception capability was filtered by a human perspective countenance. During his time spent, his sentence as it were, on planet designated earth, he could only recognize what had been previously recognized and catalogued in the human realm; his body, his mind, his clothing and varied personal accouterments thereto; his varied personal collections of odds and ends intended to please him in numerous physical surroundings of residency, neighborhood, otherwise designated localities; tools of his daily manners and trades. So, it lingered quite possible everyone and everything he experienced resided in the shade of a large abundance of misconception and poor direction imposed upon by others of his encounters from parents, neighbors, teachers, students, profession masters, and workers and business heister's, all summoned by political entities domestic and foreign whose countenance and counsel served only and merely to indulge their own tastes, greed, and otherwise devious presentation of palatable gifts and curses for profit of mind, body, soul. He came to realize a "mindbodysoul" beast resided upon and within us both visible, invisible, and otherwise at times.

He took walking trips around the grounds, outside of the house, then the further away grounds to familiarize himself with the environment and terrain. At first all seemed calm and content, but the vagaries of nature and the house origins began to assert themselves upon his physical and spiritual being. The walk stimulated his spiritual countenance but betrayed a dullness of physical acuity. He noted such a status in him stared as opposite to his younger days.

He started to pursue walks around the outer parts of the house, the exterior, in circular motion, to review and gauge the outer structure further, more so than his initial inspection before buying the house, and he began to notice nuances hidden from his first view perspective. For instance, he stepped on a piece of old gum. It stuck to his shoe. He sat along the edge of a cement sidewalk curb to scrape it off, but hidden ants invaded from a cavern point came up from the ground and started to bite and sting his ankles at the streets edge through the socks on his lower leg portions. He struggled to shake them off, then spied a nearby house spicket and ran the water, a bit rust colored, over his lowers legs to remove the ants.

On a further walk, he stepped upon an incredibly old and not noticeably short rusty nail. He heard the puncture squeegee sound as the nail embedded itself into his shoe heel. He struggled to remove the insulant and stubborn nail. Eventually, broke a portion of his right index finger-nail as unjust reward at completion of the urban project.

Still further from the grounds of his journey origin, his shoe steps expressed a weary attraction for varied mysterious ground holes, whether while on a dirt path or gravel walkway or cement sidewalk conformity, masked from his walking angle perspective, which resulted in him almost turning his ankles. He wondered of the fate and cause for these moment encounters. Many of the paths, he discovered, were variously marked by thin metal signs about an arm's length long. The signs, either color of white or green displayed odd names. He presumed, from his many travel experiences, the names either referred to historical residents, or historical moments in time, or perhaps even names of the financers or builders of such community workings. He wondered if any books had been written about the names attributed to varied streets in the numerous neighborhoods which might provoke context in the naming process. He made a note to search for such a reference book in the future as means to untie the Gordian knot of it all.

Further into the outer grounds he found unmarked paths, or at least formerly marked, as the markers had deteriorated, or became disappeared by the woodlands overgrowth which even broached upon the broken portions of the trail he spied ahead. He put off exploring these areas, turned around, but temptation called, and the now available time of an older and less frequent and flexible work schedule allowed him a block of time to traverse upon this unknown to him world. "Once a salesman always a salesman," as a mantra struck his thoughts. A prospect may loom even in these remote environs.

After walking a while into the unknown land, the unmarked paths tortured his emotions, reinvigorated memory injuries. He continued onward, pushed the memories into the darkness of his mind, and continued forward in the direction yet unreasoned of specific purpose, until he heard a sound recognizable as human in voice, although a noticeably young one according to his heart string tug. Just outside the overgrowth wall of greenery, he noticed movement amidst the brush, spotted a light skin color young hand poke through, then a white and red striped dress of horizontal alignment, adorning a young girl of perhaps 11 or 12. He tried to mask his shock at the sight of her figure, as he didn't want to frighten her, especially if she was lost and needed assistance of guidance. He expected along this portion of the pass he was more likely to transgress the property range of a groundhog or squirrel or rabbit. As he approached closer to her, his steps seemed to equal two of hers in length, and thus his approach became closer to her figure.

But as the path narrowed of woodland intrusion from each side, and as his distance from her dwindled, he became able to identify a glint of hair under a brownish head scarf. The glint revealed a gray color. The female figure turned around, and at that moment he noticed the swish of a black shawl swirl outward from the figure's neck, as the manner in which a flamingo extends wings on the cusp of a flight alignment. An elderly woman's face ame into view among the cloth accouterments and sprung upon him a woe is me type facial expression. He stopped so as not to arouse further fear in her demeanor. She softly murmured perhaps outdated wisdoms in a chant type of tone. The sounds marked wisdom, but his recognition of the word usage escaped a mental grasp. "Different wisdoms for different generations," he surmised. He looked away briefly to help quell any fear in her visage, then he looked back at her direction, and she remained no longer there. He approached where she had stood, and saw small shoe prints, but he had not noticed her shoes, so he wasn't sure if she had been there just now, or some other time, or perhaps even at all. "Time to turn back now," he said out loud, to the woodlands.

On his trek back to the house, he invariably reminisced about his past times of life moments. A young love came to mind, perhaps inspired by who he thought he saw on the woodland path. When young, about 10 or 11, he fell in love as a child falls in love, upon first sight of a classmate whom he knew nothing about except her sterile aroma, long blonde hair, and light blue eyes. He loved her but he didn't know what was love. Too afraid to speak to her, he listened to her voice which he compared to angelic given his Roman Catholic studies in elementary school where they each inhabited the same classroom as 40 other children of their age group. He tried to remember a name to match her face. "Kim, Kim was her name," he reminded himself. The spark to a candle and the spark to a firecracker could lead to different results. They were by chance seated next to each other, closely, due to the large number of students enrolled in the same class. Only for a few months this time period of their together time lasted. Other than a "hi" and "how are things going" type of conversation, they directed their attentions to the Teacher, as required, since they would have been separated if the rules were not followed properly. After only a few months, she no longer came to her desk seat in the mornings. Her family had moved away. The flame for her burned hard and deep inside him for a few years, until like all flames, the candle wick could no longer manage a spark allowance. A "goodbye" was never available, and sometimes that result is the best of situations in the human bonding cycle.

Still, his curiosity drove in his mind a specific desire to at least determine what happened. He began to hang on the outskirts of the girl groups at recess and overheard in their conversation the location where Kim lived. It was a house less than a block from the school. The girls allowed him to follow along on their walk home from school at the end of the day. They pointed out to him the house where Kim lived. He spied it from the sidewalk, not twenty feet from the door. He walked toward it, tried to remember each step, as he was in her life space, and he felt her presence as a remembrance of what he felt when sitting next to her in school. He alighted the two concrete steps to the cement porch, reached out his left arm, then pushed the doorbell button to hear the ring. It rang. Sounds of verbal fencing crashed an echo inside his skull. On the way along the walking journey to the house, the girls had told him about loud voices in the house when Kim lived there. Kim never explained to them what it was all about.

He knew of such sounds from the bowels of his own residence, one much like Kim's in appearance. And then the memories became too harsh for him. Spital sounds and hot blushed faces battered his mind, too reminiscent of his childhood spectatorship of confrontational household adults. Why angry, why nasty words filling the air, he often wondered. No answers ever revealed themselves. Fist punched and pocked drywall surfaces captured shadows casted by a fading sunlight floating through a back porch window at the back of the house of Kim. A beast of the woods he thought, sure of nature, yet able to parry in a conversational tone, who came to realize this boy is lost in this place, despite how much as a man encapsulated by a memory loop argued otherwise. Outside of the back window of the house, the land rose upwards, and he swore he could see woodland creatures of fairies-like or gnome-like in appearance according to his youthful perception abilities, and these beings coaxed him to focus better so as to further perceive their physical nature. But he had to get home or suffer the consequences of absence. So, he left the front porch of Kim's house, but the memories left with him in a shirt pocket pressed against the just outside part his chest at the heartbeat, for a long time.

His thoughts proceeded thusly in another futile attempt to forever purge them from memory during the walk to home. Then he remembered what he was not supposed to remember, that Kim said some words to him once and he didn't understand what they meant. "I need an operation. Then I will be okay." He recalled he had wondered about what she meant by these words. He didn't ask her about them. He was too shy, and too enamored of her beauty to act or ask otherwise. He too remembered her stature compared to his. He was short, and she was shorter. The most beautiful living creature he had ever encountered in life. Gone. Gone, but not truly forgotten by him. Her memory had laid dormant in his mind, stored away, lost in the old memory bins. What had preceded this moment quickly became irrelevant. Whether he could permanently banish them remained solemn conjecture. Music, of varied types, paraded his mindset towards the deep mind pit.

You live your life. You make your memories. Then, try to remember them for a long, long time. The catch is that time is short. Just short enough to make it not long enough. Always one more moment, word, touch, sound of life, breath. Fleeting lived all, and none lived fleeting. The memories you could see, like old black and white movie theater projections. They haunted. They haunted more. And they hunted, last. To learn more meant to suffer the regret of not knowing soon enough.

He heard sounds of a human voice whisper. At first, tones like a child's whimsical syllabic oblations massaged his ear cavities. Then a bit louder in volume, like a teen but uttered insolent and against the world in tone, they invaded his mind Further in sound volume similar to that of an opera soprano or tenor proceeded as if in turn. He reminded himself out loud, "Manage your senses, you must, if you are to find the hope and stamina required to solve the riddle of life." Finally, nature sounds began a chime, seemed to arouse a noise interpretable as applause in response to the vocalized sound blasts. His imagination's intensity of interjection he could not contain, even if he tried, as a density of thought projections walled in the creature of creativity his mind tended to visit. The wind around him orchestrated as conductor of the noise ensemble.

"These events are surely hauntings, unwilling to ignore my presence," he surmised. His internal voice reminded, "Master them you must, or perish quietly, alone on the plains of eternal ignorance." His mind raced in rapid thought steps. Many directions beckoned for potential sanctuary, yet his inability to choose exposed him to further audible, if only to him, haunts.

"Respighi, please rescue me with your orchestrations," he pleaded to the winds. But Hamerik upped the tempo in Symphony No. 6 Spirituelle/Allegro Molto Vivice".

Such imposition of sentence, the punishment, he feared for most of his life moments. Guilt over the simplest of indiscretions, perpetrated of innocent mind or otherwise, bashed his psyche as sledgehammer sullen.

"Ah, Bach! What have you now planned for my ears to hear?"

The moments accumulated grand, captured in memory scenes. Deny them a stage and suffer the wrath of repetitive errors. The human animal sometimes existed as a plague upon itself, by means of a capture of senses attached to memories and eventually attacked by regrets. Happier moments interceded but remained insufficient to quench the eternal thirst for more senses stimulation.

During these memory haunts, he lost all feeling in his body, as if it didn't exist. A purple starling outside the window tapped lightly some matter of concern unknown to him. He couldn't identify where he existed, either in spot or time moment, or how he had arrived there, or whether his reality had been infected by some communicable virus. Only his brain seemed to work at the moment, so he continued on a search to identify his temporary physical paralysis.

A vision of the mysterious woman served as newest plague. "She has her carpenter. I have my soul. All is right with the world, for a few moments, anyway." Temporary solace still counted as such, or each, or maybe neither. Little victories multiplied wide, hoe the garden from side to side. Don't fear the reaper. It doesn't fear you. Miracles happen. Snow falls. Defeats roll, and slide, and stall. Pluck the banjo, slide the violin. Sometimes the door swings out and sometimes in. His last thought coaxed back to a first thought.

If it doesn't taste like a smooth beer, or hold tight like a finely wrapped stogie, or sway hips like a mature willow tree, not interested.

Tchaikovsky's "The Seasons: March", interceded on his behalf, as a contemplative mind tone began to overtake his assignations.

The nature around him resisted his mental gymnastics avoidance, and proceeded in tune of mimic, as Chopin's "Waltz No.6 in D Flat", also known colloquially as "Minute Waltz". One minute could make all of the difference, should it enter the time stage on cue.

The flitters he feared. A friend of his, when they were young together in age, had referred or nicknamed his sudden mind drops of random, unconnected senses and sensations as such. Much like a candle flicker they were, except of the mind in origin, filtered down to vocal cords, then mouthed in flitters. Could clear a room of humans. Perhaps their purpose, as housed, or interred in his soul.

"Yes. Must be the flitters. Still, they haunt me."

There was a time when the insect world slayed his interest, then puberty struck hard into his chest, and all manner of cogent thought gradually subsided into the mush of emotion. He often wondered why he found it so difficult to embrace others, when their physical inclination identified a need for such action. Just the thought of such action rang repugnant to his senses. He gladly embraced use of his other senses in such moments, particularly smell.

Smell seemed to rule him at varied times. The other senses stoked a spark of fear in his heart. Not necessarily at the beginning portion of the activity, but at the conclusion of it. He worried of the loneliness disease even though his outward personality dictated a need otherwise. Perhaps relatives older than him, who seemed to overtly engorge at the hug moments, required such times to engage and feast upon the activity as means to satiate their own fears while ensconced in a comfort blanket. He never felt comfortable as someone else's blanket.

The transmission of varied bodily excrements, as breath, spittle, cosmetics transfer, hair contact, clothing entanglements and the overall frictions of the moment extensively caused his body to exert a monkish demeanor out of a self-preservation need to propel away from such motions and emotes. He simply feared physical expression of his own emotive actions as he remained completely unable to gauge the repercussions of such upon the party who initiated the hug invasion. That was it. He felt his soul stir negative at the thoughts of such demand in these friction events. In the times when a hug was thrust upon him, he could feel his energy drain straight away, as if all feeling inside of him had been uncovered and prepared ready for immediate inspection, or carted away in the aftermath of the embrace, never to be seen again, as a walking child snatched on the streets, or persuaded away at a playground by an untoward passerby.

These moments added up into him, as rocks piled high on a beach, or bricks laid to form building structures. The pigeons would land upon him and drip their excrement, and he would remain stuck, imprisoned there unable to escape or wipe away the mess. There cannot be much comfort in life when the next movement of a nearby human evokes fear at an ever-increasing level on the discomfort meter.

His fear of such human contact, closeness, caused him to expend much energy shielding himself from the discomfort. He genuinely tried to understand his fear, the reason for it, the cause, but a cure eluded his intellectual grasp, even into years beyond youth. As a result, he was labelled quickly as someone possessed of a short attention span. He couldn't help it. Too much wit from a seasoned mind taxed his brain to the point of exhaustion. He needed time to rest of thought machinations.

In elementary school, his moments called into service by a teacher, to deliver oral instructions to another teacher in another classroom down the hall usually resulted in his failure to deliver a complete or accurate message. In this case, the Homeroom class was instructed they would complete artwork to demonstrate what occupation they wanted to pursue when they grew up. He was sent down the hall to the primary Art teacher's room to collect some paste jars, construction paper, and number two pencils for his Homeroom teacher's Art class, but he failed to remember all three necessary items. So, first he asked only for the paste jars, as he couldn't remember the other items. Upon return to his Homeroom, the teacher sent him back in a hint of admonishment voice, for to collect the construction paper and number two pencils. He came and went on his next mission, but upon return, only brought back the construction paper.

Now his Homeroom teacher expressed concern on the cusp of an exasperation tone, and the directed admonishment reverberated in his skull as a well-read and voiced tome a bit louder, enough so for the other students to cease their work amidst dins of self-indulgent creative joy tasks. He then trekked to the Art teacher's room again to collect, somewhat sullen in mannerisms, what was it, oh, the Art teacher reminded him he must be working on that special project his Homeroom teacher had mentioned to her last week, then he was provided the number two pencils. Upon returning to Homeroom with the last correct artwork tool he immediately was instructed to hurry up as most of the class had completed all but the drawing portion of the project. He commenced in earnest to his work desk area, used his number two pencil to draw a policeman, as it was the first human figure he could think of for this project called "create artwork using paste, construction paper, and a pencil".

Scissors would be needed but they were never taken out of the Homeroom as their permanent place was in teacher's locked supply cabinet and use of such metal implements was only issued with permission. He realized he needed scissors when he saw his classmates had already cut out their cardboard strips and pasted them together on the theme tablet provided by Homeroom teacher. The students only needed to draw any picture they chose onto the tablet paper. He decided he would ask for the scissors usage after he drew his picture. He was about to draw his picture on the construction paper at his desk, but realized he had to decide what job he wanted. He started on his original thought, policeman, but while drawing, thought of other occupations.

The other students seemed to already have decided on character amidst discussion he was unable to overhear as he had commenced so many trips to acquire project materials. Policeman, like the father of one of his neighbors? Shoe repairer, like his maternal grandfather? Furniture maker, like his fraternal grandfather? He had mostly completed a drawing after much erasure as his thoughts of the other occupations translated onto the construction paper during the process. He realized he was supposed to draw on the theme tablet, but it was too late now to stop. So, he had a policeman, holding a shoe, looking at small wooden beams which floated around the male clothed figure. He finished the male figure, the school bell rang, and it was break time.

He wasn't allowed to go on break because he didn't finish his project. So, he alone remained behind, watched by the art teacher who had come to the Homeroom to collect the art tools she had provided. She didn't seem happy to be asked to stay and watch him during the break, as she would have been on her break. He remembered the cackling she spouted to no one in particular, as the echo of it bounced off the walls and ceiling of the now lonely classroom, except for her and little him. He hurried to finish so he could make his escape outside to the happy banter of first recess, but he struggled in the theme tablet paper cutting needed to make a frame for his drawing, and further struggled with the pasting as his paste jar top was stuck shut due to glue left on the outer edges of the lid, not previously wiped dry, before the last user screwed the lid back on.

He was afraid to ask the already disgruntled Art teacher for assistance, so he left everything as it was, and lied when the teacher asked, "are you finished yet?" because recess was more important to him than pasting paper together. She let him leave, but when he returned he received a sound scolding in the hallway from his Homeroom teacher, audible to all of his classmates as they sat and waited for his scolding to end. His Homeroom teacher's voice strolled down the halls of the entire floor as if her voice attempted to alert every classroom of his indiscretions of the last half hour plus. In less than an hour he managed to discombobulate the minds of his Homeroom teacher, Art room teacher, classmates, and other teachers who proceeded to demand their classroom doors be shut to avoid the ignominious din served up by his Homeroom teacher's well-constructed tirade moment. He still had to worry about his dad finding out, which meant another scolding, and the disappointed scowl and raised in anger Italian accented voice of his mom over the embarrassment she would suffer amidst her social acquaintances when they heard of his unforgivable error of "inability to follow instructions". His Art project picture wasn't taped to the hallway walls like the pictures of his classmates because his project was marked "incomplete".

The admonishments of his parents piled high vociferously over his young years in the forms of "pay attention", "follow instructions", "write things down and memorize them". He doggedly attempted to follow their advice, and in the doing of it, became the best Artist in the final elementary level class. He still now retained the gold-colored Art Award pin presented to him upon graduation. He kept it in a small cedar box, and from time to time, when reminiscences became important as reminders of struggles and victories, he would open the box, finger the pin and some of the other memory relics, to remind of the moments he had achieved a level of recognized competence as reward after suffering the rigors of failure and persistent strains of betterment efforts.

Random thoughts proceeded to torture him as intermittent thunderstorms. His first sexual encounter completely destroyed his previous life of casual physical innocence, and he became reincarnated amidst an insatiable thirst, never completely satisfied. A curse it was. A curse. The curse of human adulthood painted black. A wicked creature, it roamed mad in the deepest caverns of the human soul.

Nothing spoiled a meal like the first taste. The remainder of the journey rode downhill into belly aches and digestive twists and turns like the roller coaster from hell. Sounds and smells deflated the pleasant joy of that first taste, sip, smell, until all other delicacies of life eroded into rote and repetitive displeasures. The human condition played out more like a prison sentence.

After he finished the journey of feeling sorry for himself, he began the journey again, as all journeys began since forever, at the first step. Only oblivion awaited. Along the oblivion path, he learned from the example of those around him there may be a means of coping along the journey. It was too early to give in and fall to the temptations and potholes. Miracles existed everywhere even if not readily visible to him. In books, in words written and spoken, in imagination, in science, a purpose could be gleaned with little more than token effort. A spark existed out there in the ether, in the everywhere, somewhere, for his connected senses to become ignited into purpose whether accidental or intended.

And so, his next journey purpose evolved into a search for a clearer defined journey, to find a worthy path as expression of humanity's gift, in a world pock-marked of inhumanity. Billions of other humans had been commissioned to trudge the same path. Many footprints formed in the muck. Many directions determined to follow. Search. Search. Connect innate interests, from whatever course ignited, to reveal an identifiable purpose.

Of necessity, he jumped over many fences into the plaintive yards of possibility. Chased by dogs, tweeted harshly by birds, zeroed in upon by multitudes of insects and kamikaze bugs. Such was the human journey, from bear cub to full blown grizzly. True or false. Real or not. Fair or foul. Nice or creepy unkind. The gamut of life darts played their directed and misdirected course upon his body, mind, and soul to the usual crossroads: retreat, stop, charge forward into the lightning storm. Bumps, bruises, wounds skin deep or deeper toiled at his being.

The most difficult task involved development of trust. He never came close to mastering it. Always a heartbreak involved. Too many heart-breaks will do that to a human, whether they are self-inflicted through carelessness or senselessness, or inflicted by birthed origins hurled as spears by other humans whose wheels had been broken upon their own paths. Or inflicted by media and marketing outlets. Yet, there always re-mained a choice, of find another path, and thus suffer the ousting of one's faux safety amidst the birth culture. Such a debacle faced many souls. Stay as trained, or seek better environs, more suitable to the con-science.

The first and most important test remained to identify personal strengths and weaknesses, temptations, learn to master control of them, then forge ahead as a stone solid creature, unchained from societal ex-pectations. Masks of smile or frown, appropriately used, and cloth cos-tumes of conventional norms helped serve as a protective outer shell to serve as means to navigate the rough patches. And perspective. Media wasn't honest, down to the last syllable of communication. Never trusted it, after long periods of trusting blindly, only to learn the harsh reality of deceits inflicted. Many products purchased which didn't live up to the hype, even endangered one's physical functions. Always things to never trust outright existed either in plain sight or cloaked in dark shadows. Such a perspective of open trust loomed as the false step, waiting to break upon the foot path at any time.

The humans and manufactured implements, their names faded, but not their faces and facades. The faces became a wicked dark garden that festered solid in his mind. Sometimes he couldn't even close his eyes to capture some rest from the faces. Like tenpins bowling bowls they rolled their weight into his mind, his closed eyesight unable to dodge their sound and fury presence, devious smirks. He forced himself to find memories of pleasant times stored away in the brain for such moments of challenge. He abhorred medications reliance's, for some were humans alliances, as they trapped him into the blackness void. And yet the RX curse loomed large and unholy upon the human tapestry. The medical pill was advertised as a mercy, but mercy many times proved as medication prescribed by the devil.

The written word world of 500 years served a noble purpose, helped spread knowledge far and wide upon the earth's surface, but along with enshrined wisdom had also birthed devious lies, misconceptions in equal measure. The big tech world boasted no such moral equivalence. Manipulation of facts, twisting of truths, invention of lies seeded the indoctrination protocol of humans, took on a whole new meaning and level of deviance.

Lesser creatures used such tactics to acquire food as nourishment, and so too, humans learned similar tactics. The primary tool was the spoken word, then the written, then a combination of both written and spoken words. Tech advances like radio, television, internet, and more provided ample opportunity for a mass population poisoning. The world had become poisoned dead many times over. Now was just the latest addiction recovery time period. The poison became easier to taste when hidden in a beautiful oral or readable presentation. He lived at this time period, when a horrible revelation revealed itself to him.

Technology had raised humankind to new heights. That same technology could serve to push humankind back into the earth, crushed into seedlings, more acutely trapped at the mercy of nature and weather currents, because any opportunity survival existed as foil for the resonance of continuation purpose. Foil as fancy, or fancy as foil. For as much as humans attempted to wrestle, capture the golden goose, they merely had enslaved themselves to eternal grief, intermittent regrets, and solemn resignations. Ultimately, all life moments served as settlement of existence contraptions. "Deal with it," he reminded himself, regularly, at moments random, or events planned.

Did they, the politicians, the educators, think we did not need our freedom? Was it merely a commodity for them to buy and sell, to offer loans for payback with interest, then market to us again as composed of lesser quality ingredients, for their own profit? They convinced us we didn't really need it, not in the degrees attained, that we could lend it to them, and they would give it right back with interest, as they would take care of it for us, after acquiring it, then dole back out in doses equal for everyone, after they took a large portion of it as their cut. The bamboozle deluxe package they marketed. Our very existence fueled their greed.

Exposure to lies and propaganda were many in the pre big tech days, but once big tech became slave masters, all humanity sunk deep into the bog of brain manipulation. Big tech became a beast, bent on purging thoughts not acceptable to the mind slave masters. Now noble meant devious. Right meant wrong. Happy meant sad. Free meant enslaved. Detractors of such a life were shunned from society as pariahs of insensibility. Only tyrants ruled such lands. Only the unwanted voices were slit at the throat of sound.

Thoughts had become fishing hooks for the big tech world. Whoever controlled the tech controlled the world of human thoughts. Once they acquired enough power and reach, there was no stopping them. Too much power and control were never enough. The human condition writ large upon the intellectual landscape became attached by their chains. We merely served as their plow horses.

All must concede to their influence and power, or else. Their advertising was pleasant and enticing and inescapable. Their influence purpose was enslavement. Pay the toll or become irrelevant. Divide and conquer had become perfected, and not a sword, or cannonball, or bullet required need to shepherd the human herd into a land of forever enslavement. Too much is never enough stalked new meaning.

He imagined a race of people named "Dracians", mythical peoples who could conquer all, and once their conquests ended, after engulfing and ingesting anything and everything, they proceeded to do the same to themselves, as they were a mix of varied ethnic clans, and one by one they broke off into groups and consumed themselves, at the behest of their politicians who grew powerful, fat, and lazy of all around them except holding onto their own power.

Journey First Steps

His long vehicle imbued road trip had finally reached the intended destination. After mentally boxing his imaginations and fancies, and carefully driving upon a parking lot that peered back at him more so as an abandoned utility fixture, he exited the vehicle and proceeded along the path of his plan. A sign for "Real Reality" noted for him the correct destination had been achieved. The door opened itself electronically upon recognition of his human presence approaching. He wondered if dogs or larger animals could elicit the same effect, in nearness presence.

Upon entry to the interior, somewhat cooled in climate, pleasingly so according to reactions of his exposed skin at the face and hands, he noticed her blue name tag, pinned to a lighter blue blouse.

"Well, Ms. Dorinda K., glad to meet you."

She looked up at him, after shuffling the white papers pocked full of tiny letters. She seemed not as nearly settled, in demeanor, as he.

"So, what did you do for a living?" she asked politely.

"Varied things," he responded, as intention to appear mysterious.

"Perhaps most notable," she asked in a somewhat forced jovial tone.

"I invented a machine that permits a person to identify their own scent, at various stages of their day or week or month. It varies, you know."

"I didn't. Know, I mean," she responded, still polite in tone.

"Of course. Well, perhaps my marketing left something to be desired," he expressed in a conciliatory tone.

"Well, regarding your tenancy here . . . "

"Tenacity?" he blurted quizzically.

"No, tenancy," she said.

"Oh, yes, of course tenancy." Apparently he misunderstood her intentions, then he continued on upon his invention explanation path. "I added a machine feature, for a price, that allowed owners to identify a scent most compatible to their own, for relationships, business trips, things of that social nature. Experimented with animal scents, dogs, cats, to determine cross species compatibility, between pets and animals and humans, but some of the experiments went awry, some lawsuits involved, adverse reactions, etc., and etc.," he rambled a bit loudly.

"I can imagine," she agreed.

"So, I sold off the business entity. Now only farmers and hunters use a downgraded version of the product."

"Genuinely nice," she offered as concession to his little diatribe.

"Eventually. Took a while, to recover, straighten things out," he offered, calming a bit in demeanor.

His mental humiliation scars from the experiments acted up, bit a sting at his psyche. He began rubbing them through his clothing in varied places of his anatomy. He hoped this desk jockey worker didn't notice his discombobulation. "Of course, she noticed," he thought. He noticed she checked a small clock on her desk.

"I have a few sample bottles of the product if you'd like some," he offered as rote apology.

"Oh, thanks, but no, no. Perhaps save it for someone, or something else," she politely responded in the manner of a dedicated businessperson intent on completing the tasks for which she earned adequate compensation.

He wondered if he was taxing her mission, but he remained yet to become stymied. His salesmanship craft developed over many hills, dales, and years of toil had created an immunity to the varied daggers of sharpness rejection.

Stilled, he understood her perspective. The topic died a cruel but quick death, mercifully, from his perspective. It appeared to him that her work perspective sounded like a continuous drumbeat of Chopin Mazurka's, one after another and another, until break or lunch time. Judging by the hour on her clock, which displayed time from both sides, her vision views and his, one or the other of break or lunch approached ad nauseam, and she appeared in a near rabid state, exuded into the room by glint of her eyes. He wanted to avoid her glance, and she obliged, reciprocated, perhaps due to his incessant clothing rub sounds.

To break the ice, he remarked in a jovial tone, "I wish to remain here until my end days, and beyond." He laughed at his last expression of thought "and beyond". The real estate young lady seemed to take this jovial comment in passing as a factual statement. A rogue wind gusted near the side window, whistled through the frame.

"Wish granted," she stated, matter of factly.

"Thank you for joining the game," he remarked with a smile chaser.

Then she smiled and looked him in the face, into his eyes, as if she had casted an enchantment upon him, and spoke, "You've done some acting. I can tell."

"Yes. My true aspiration," he said, but he feared his own eye gleam betrayed a full purpose of conviction. He smiled again. She continued speaking, in an instructional tone this time.

"Just some important reminders. There is a marsh at the north end of the house, about 100 yards away, and it emits quite a bit of foggy residue in that portion of the property. It is not recommended to travel in that area alone, or at all really, as the ground isn't stable afoot, given the dampness of that area.

"Will remember. Thanks," he noted vociferously.

"Always in that condition, potentially," she said, then continued on, "In summertime, it pretty much dries up, but the dampness is so deep and dense, the surface may look completely dry and yet gobble up the feet and legs of a traveler. There have been stories, in these parts."

"Stories?" he wondered aloud.

"Yes. Of travelers who stayed at the house, when it was a partial bed and breakfast briefly at the turn of the last century . . ."

"Yes, yes, go on. What stories?" he interrupted, as urged from her response.

"Of missing traveler's, who left early, without checking out first or paying the bill. Never seen or heard from again. Except for one."

"Well, sounds like a local legend to capture curious souls and visitors into the area, as sort of a macabre mystery tour." He wondered about the one traveler who remained immune to the bed and breakfast spell.

The clock alarm on the real estate lady desk began a rhythmic ding. After five short dings it stopped.

"Well, where did the time go? she grasped a tone by the throat.

"Same place it always goes. Away," he trailed her exposition, with a soft laugh.

"Lunch for me. Here are your papers. Call if you need anything."

He didn't know who to call or by what means as she didn't provide a name, and there was no phone equipment on or around her desk to serve as a wire connection. Perhaps a mobile phone she used.

She scooted out a door hinged into the wall behind her, it closed calmly shut, and he remained there in the lobby, alone, except for the paperwork in front of him on the top of the wooden, perhaps walnut, desk. He looked at the top page. A business card beamed at him in the face of his just exited hostess. Her name and mobile number appeared in special, raised ink print, for easy viewing. Impressed by what appeared to be an engraved card where the type appeared on it, he lifted his right hand, extended his index finger, and touched the printed portion, slid his finger across it, and noticed a honeysuckle scent enter the air near his nostrils. "Seems someone became enamored of my invention efforts."

He drove to the house of his recent purchase, at least, he must have, since he found himself staring at it from the edge of a gray stone driveway the width of two automobiles. He reminded himself, as means to shatter a fear of lost memory, many times, the eyes see what the mind wants them to see. In looking at the house exterior, of high and long appearance, long ago memories flooded his mind. The memories paralyzed his physical movements, as the memories projected a past he had tried to forget. A soliloquy commenced in tune with his mindset.

"She forced me to discover things about her, instead of just telling what she wanted. Forced was a bit of a harsh word, as her beauty, her smell, her voice had captured me as willing participant in magical moment machinations, such as laughs, smiles, hugs, hand holds, hair strums, conversations about life, love, hopes, dreams, all of unending possibility.

She provided clues of her interest, through the meals she created. Her enchiladas made it easy to surrender. Smells deep, sounds of crunch and slurp, food colors light brown-orange-red-green, presentation stately, things like that. But I never quite grasped her deepest and entire meanings. At least, I sensed so.

Eventually, I became bored by the unsolved mystery of her essence, and she became bored by repetitive presentation of clues unsolvable to my mind efforts. So, our paths diverged, separated completely except for corollary co-habitation, of economic necessity. Then she discovered greener pastures, after intentional searches, and I was gone from her life in body, mind, and spirit, but not in bank account. She picked that clean as a vulture picks through a desert carcass. Such indignant appreciation actions perpetrated by her scourged my heart. I never really became able to forgive her, so I forgot her. It was easier to forget, or at least bury her images alive in the deepest part of my soul. The soul is a graveyard of many depths and expanses, can hold much baggage, corpses of life moments, but I learned the hard way, such wounds can never become fully healed or hidden from the soul mirror. The memories attached to her, our times together, and apart, stung like the wasp needle. Upon which moment chosen, at random, in moments of silence or introspection, an invasion of heart stings loomed still possible, regardless of time passages."

He so learned every moment of solace was proceeded by many moments of sorrow, and the solace moments only portended future moments of sorrow. Echoes of the hell caverns reverberated amidst the music of the heavens. No moment was spared by the eyes and ears and nose of human conscience.

"Key reist's sake, will it ever end, the circumspection?"

"You took the name, poorly, of the savior, in vain."

"Feck you!" the old woman on the other side of the tree line spouted. He didn't know who she was, but there was plenty of time to learn. At least her voice wrenched him from the grasp of memories poor in spirit. He judged the voice amidst the tree line as a woman, old in age, of unkind attitude, perhaps because he was yet unknown to her, and so posed a threat to any solitude she had gained from the comfort of nothing changed in her life for some time. Comfort in routine. He could see the value is such a circumstance if it happened at the appropriate time in a life.

She inspired him to learn more about his new neighborhood. Opportunities should arise when talking with residents nearby and somewhat further away, until he felt comfortable in this new world. Perhaps there were other towns nearby and ready for exploration. His wonder had been piqued.

Are some residents former caretakers of his newfound property? Guardians, or even guards, for that matter, of the boundary lines which segregated the sacred fairy-like entranced land from the usual human, animal, insect, vegetation world? His imagination took off wildly on this matter of thought.

Would he eventually learn why no one ever purchased the property long ago, or why it was zoned for residential use until 200 years or so ago? Perhaps because of the strange effects the soil and land perpetrated upon anyone who moved around in the environment there. Maybe an intoxication of mind, which somewhat paralyzed the humans and animals, and god knows what other creatures may live on the other side of the tree line, amidst shadows there, or far down the long and winding dirt road path he could see as it disappeared into a thick area of great oaks.

He now found himself inside his new residence, at the mercy of a large front hall in size, bedazzled by many and high bookshelves, still harboring books readied for intellectual stimulation journeys. Echoes of his shoes scraping upon the wooden floor entry hallway had yet to rest from his mind jolts.

He realized once settled in, he needed to sit by the first-floor bay window, or up high on the second floor, and spy the tendencies of the squirrels, birds, even insects, to determine any oddities outside of his normal realizations of such creature activities. These ruminations set him a bit dizzy and off balance. He searched for a chair, and found one appropriate for rest, next to a small table, already adorned by a half-glass full on wine, stationed quite restful next to a cellophane wrapped large cigar. His real estate agent must have presented such a surprise, as congratulations for occupancy upon the property.

After resting his bum upon the single cushion chair seat and relaxing his upper body at the spinal column of his back against the broad and high and pleasantly soft, not too stiff chair back, he began an analysis of whether he should break some old habits. Not necessarily to kill them, but perhaps moderate them in frequency or intensity. For now, a sweet wine sip from a clean glass, a robust cigar stem tucked between his lips and readied for a lighter ignition, and a comfortable chair stationed towards a scoping look outward of the bay window served adequate purpose. Finally, the pleasant sound of Gluck's "Dance Of The Blessed Spirits/Orpheus And Eurydice" fluted by James Galway worked simply fine in all manners and fashions he could hope to imagine.

Plenty of time to bury old memories sour and observe the creation of new ones sweet. He could imagine himself no more fortunate after so much of life lived than this special moment granted to him. "You've got your life. I've got mine. The two shall never again intertwine." He wasn't sure if these words came from his mind or another's. They served equal in purpose, on the whole.

His mind traveled into the woods, either of course in memory or actual intent current, he would determine later, but the heading was set, and his body traveled upon the ding. Squirrels chirped and eyed his maneuvers. His clothing scraped against something in the woods when he went off trail to explore. A dim light beckoned in his sight, glowing a temptation of closeness, as the sun traveled downward for daylight needed rest. Off the edge of the walking trail what came into his view appeared a small and quaint house perhaps stationed here to essentially escape the world, after occupation retirement or some unfortunate course of events.

After viewing the glow, it apparently came towards him and provided happy feelings inside his chest while appearing to massage his skin, touch him in varied places on his body, like a sexually stimulated woman's touch of hand and further skin to body accoutrements. The feeling declined as it left him and disappeared towards the horizon, amidst tree foliage, but after he arrived home, and for the next few days, he noticed feeling increases and recedes in varied parts of his house, also outside when he walked around the property and explored further the forested woods nearby. Such feelings mirrored his own physical symptoms mysterious. "Sometimes life's too short to sew a rip in the pants," he counseled. "Dodge and parry. Dodge and parry." The squirrels had learned such lessons long, long ago. They resided eons heavy of wisdom.

On one of his later walking trips, through patches of thick woodland growth, his vision came set upon a little girl adorned in a light blue dress, alone in the forest. He wondered how she had arrived there in a spot tight with woodlands overgrowth. Her dress exhibited no evidence of brush or branches foliage contact inevitable in such a place, no tears, no streaks, but refused, he did, an immediate wander of mind about the circumstance. The wander overcame his mind quickly.

Suspicions aroused, given his age and experience, something didn't seem right and good in the moment. Her visage exhibited not a touch of fear or dread. Her voice tone, a whisper like the brush of fingertips too light for harp strings to flush out a clear sound, yet facially confident and assured touched his ears calm as he asked her questions to determine identity and how she had arrived there. She responded in a handsy physical manner through her appearance, mimicking his concerns. Her dress appeared dirtier in the filtered light beams shooting through the trees, then he noticed her shoes, which started out looking clean, devoid of mud or dirt, but became to appear dirtier, more used. His observations of her ticked of several boxes to alleviate nefarious concerns, but then he noticed her physical appearance began to change, from radiant beauty into evidence matters of scratches, dried blood streams on legs, arms, as if having run through a thicket area of bushes. He also noticed a silence in the nature around them. No wind, no birds chirps, no other animals seemed at normal activity level. Her very appearance seemed to suspend all other living creature and nature activity. Such silence indicated the presence of a predator about the woods.

He wondered of her purpose here, as she seemed neither lost in spirit nor concerned of the circumstances. He found himself to wonder if he had entered a dream state, or had he been enchanted by some poisonous weed or flower in the brush that spouted some mysterious pollen into the wind and subsequently it had accumulated on his upper lip just below his nostrils. After a bit of dizzy feeling in his head, and weakness in his gut, he reached arms out from each side of his body to hold onto the high brush, until he could compose himself.

Once reconstituted in attention, he looked at the place where she had stood. The spot portrayed that her form had disappeared, become vanquished from his presence, by a means uncertain to him. But he could not forget her face. His last observation of her form displayed her face to have been shattered in places, the skin flaked off, shards of bone ground down, prickly broken in chipped remnants like a non-sanded two by four piece of lumbar. She had allowed him to move closer, to inspect her wounds. Amidst the mesh of facial destruction, he sensed a beauty when he imagined the shattered parts pieced back together from bone to skin, so much so, his eyes became watered, then filled of fluid, then leaked tears upon his outer nasal areas. Downward upon his cheeks they trickled, until he was relieved of their salty sting.

Now alone in the woods, reminded he became of a memory buried deep inside his psyche. It reminded of the one case he was never able to solve as an investigator. He had sought additional work when regular product sales went slow, so he pursued training and employment as an independent, given his ability to measure the motivations of customers. His work allowed him to assist short-handed Police and Sheriff agencies.

The case of the missing little girl, who was never found, lingered deep within his memory. That case stuck into his mind like a wasp stinger. While at the alleged scene of where the little girl was last known to be present, he reached out to open a white door in the house kitchen. He interpreted it as a closet door, perhaps harboring a small pantry space, but he became distracted by an odd tweet sound, emanated from the window open over top the kitchen sink. He thought of the sound as a bird chirp, perhaps cardinal, or finch, then a male voice called out, one of the police officers, and he never opened the door, his hand mere fractions of an inch from the door knob old in appearance, as if it didn't belong there, older than the room design at least, as the kitchen appeared to have been renovated and repainted several times, except this door, yellowed, stained by elements unknown to him, and the knob polished and worn by many hands of many twists over perhaps generations and generations of families in this house of about 200 years in usage.

The little girl was never found. The mystery of her disappearance, and perhaps death, was never resolved. Perhaps nature determined there was a lot of death that needed to be reconciled here, in the place where he now resided. He realized long ago the ideas which popped into his head became pieces to a mental jigsaw puzzle, but he could not pull all the necessary pieces out to form a complete picture. Many mysteries swam around in his head, sometimes like lily pads resting on pond water, interrupted by a frog jump or mosquito lay, or baby snakes' curly cue like at play.

All play and no prey led to desperate moments. Some lives too short, short, or a tad longer than short, came and went. To try and understand the paradise described by ancients and literature and music types played a false hope. No eternal place existed here. Life and death moments befell every single second and sooner during every single rise and set of the Sun star.

Have you ever been in that moment where no one else around understood what you just realized, and now know, and must tell someone about it, or maybe still, not yet tell anyone about it, because the unusual nature of it is too impossible to understand, but you take the chance, risk it, tell it, to someone. "Yeah, I know what you mean, sure. I have no clue, dude," he heard often as the bleak sortie, as the oratorical brush off hint.

Of course, this mind fleck usually happened when no one was around, and the only observers of the effect were roaches, rats, or crows. As a mind flux, it hummed. After living alone for a while, he finally realized he could pop a pickle into his face, at the mouth cavern to be specific, any time he wanted. Then he wondered, "how come I didn't?" A life change moment, he realized.

Also, after much contemplation time, he realized he'd never left a room, or a bar or tavern, while the song "Dancing Queen", by ABBA, was playing on the radio or jukebox. His feet tingled gently at such thoughts. Perhaps he had discovered the only moments when he stopped grinding his teeth together. Just trying to find his way, he supposed. "Must be this way for others, humans, too," he thought, "in their specific alone moments." His return sojourn, back towards his new house, ended. He entered.

Well, time for bed struck into his mind, softly, like that autumn leaf just floating down into an end time moment upon the lawn's grassy bed. Perhaps a moon sliver would watch downward, upon him, and of course, billions of other humans, somewhere on the planet. What big eyes it would require, to achieve such vision, such scope comprehension. Synapses would explode, or at least, become overloaded at high traffic volume intersections.

Unfortunately, another thought infected his mind, not deeply, but deep enough to begin a burrow effort. Silence he requested of the environs about his abode place and outside of it, yet crickets chirped. He lived no longer in the city, so the lack of background noise boomed into him like a loud thunder roll. He tried to distract himself into sleep, but the effort resulted in another defeat, number 13 visited upon his daily moments.

He sighed. Listened to himself sigh. Awaited it to end, the sigh, akin to the feelings of the last notes of a Chopin nocturne, which one he couldn't recall, but the notes recalled him listening, or so he thought, or imagined, or dreamed. Then he listened to the post-sigh silence, except the crickets interjected, somewhat pleasantly at this moment. Perhaps they were providing a new sound to encourage his sleep. He had yet to adjust to the low volume new noise as it echoed along the outside environs, and eventually creeped into his room.

He couldn't remember if he had left the window up. The sill beckoned, just along the right side of his vision, as he stared at the far wall, wondered what might appear on his mind screen, yet hoped nothing appeared, so as to encourage his sleep effort. "Close the eyes," he reminded. These moments of personal rumination discovery had become rare enlightenment for him. Pencil, paintbrush, knife, gun. Ultimately, his tension showed as a closed fist.

He missed the specific ignition of irritation for a while, unable to identify it until reality focus he allowed to proceed, instead of imagination focus. Note to self, "this imagination formed many of perspectives." All the experiences of his life projected upon him visions pursed by his senses which had been tested at any given moment throughout his life, from birth to death. Death. It had not yet arrived for him, he reminded. Why did he think about death? He didn't know it, except from observation of creatures, a few humans, plant life such as grass during seasonal transformations, or weeds he casted out during gardening exorcisms.

The most insidious life moments existed born of old truths, evolved into lies, then became reborn as new truths. All hinged on perspective. Perspective. The baggage of senses accumulation. Some baggage lay fresh upon the mind. Some grew stale, subjected to a late stay in the back and dark recesses of the icebox.

Sleep had begun to drug him into heavy lids and half-visible moment frames. How to distinguish real now from his perspective of now, and escape perspective's rotten clutches. Impossible? No. "Must learn to coalesce all mind functions in order to become more efficient in specific areas of moment experience and process methods."

His mind drifted upon floated hills of such thoughts. Four-legged earth creatures had accomplished such skills at early age, for purpose of survival. Humans, not as much so in progression of skill development amidst the four-legged creature world. Exposed they were to baser instincts perfection imbued to lesser living things, from the human perspective. Took a long time for the human to progress in skill development, yet once that development reached appropriate levels, no lesser creature stood a chance of survival. The only living creature still superior to human evolution remained the earth ball itself. As a whole, it was god. Controller of the land, sea, weather systems. To believe, as a human, that ultimate and complete control of each environment loomed possible, meant to believe a piss in the wind would not touch the soul of the pisser. It did involve a touch moment, after drenching the body and the cloth laid upon it in advance.

Even after sufficient mental and physical human development to survive alone was accomplished, the survival of the human against itself remained the battle. Perception, knowledge pursuits, social interactions posed still a challenge, although lesser so much depending upon skills developed along the way in societal and mechanical endeavors. Once again, senses development almost ruled all, as wall, river, cleanser, murky mud drencher. A sea of weeds looked much different depending on the standing point origin of observation. Surrounded, boundary born, outside the cage served as best place for final analysis attempt, after accumulation of multiple analysis experiences had become sorted, boxed, filed and made available for future consultation.

How many quality and noticed experiences does it take to become eminent renowned in the processing. Many. And many more. And always some more. A thirst for knowledge too strong can lead to a drowning of the mind and separation of it from the soul. How to escape such entanglements becomes the bewitched nature of the life journey.

This mind soliloquy, one he played upon himself throughout his life, almost never achieved an end. he was the one who could become dead and not even know it yet. He was the one who contemplated death so much, he became unworried by the course of it, the path, the journey. One foot in front of the other, whether that foot was imaginary or real in projection and step. A sweet child of himself, he had become. And all around him, an interceder of some degree sort. A self-conversation interceded upon his thought journey.

"When you season your food, do you use first the saltshaker or the pepper shaker?"

"Does it make a difference?"

"Some people think so."

"What people?"

"Psychologists, psychotherapists and such."

"Poker players using minds as chips, they are."

"I'll see your narcissist and raise you two hypochondriacs."

Stalemate.

"Too many voids connected disjointed puzzle pieces."

The Beast

His ears detected musical sounds like Johann Strauss, II, "Wine, Woman and Song Waltz", helped Knack dance his mind through another walk trek along the dirt paths of his new environs. Here at a crossroads of paths he met The Beast, or so it seemed to him. The creature, or man, or humanoid exhibited a quite unnatural shag of hair from the top of the head, surrounding the facial features, and trailing off at the jaw line. Otherwise, this creature displayed a manner of dressage suitable of nobility status, on two legs standing, and of great height in stature. The aroma about him seemed a bit familiar, of the acquaintance kind.

"Beast. What ails you to find need along my travel path?"

The creature seemed taken aback by the term used.

"Me? Beast? I knocked on your residence door not much time ago previous. We briefly commiserated."

Knack displayed a confused look. "Am I not seeing a Beast?" he wondered silent. Perhaps in these parts, not. And the creature could speak, although the lips draped below the nasal passages and just above a chin of overgrown hairy froths didn't appear capable of forming human-like audible or sensible sounds. Still, he seemed a bit familiar in appearance to someone he met recently. The voice sounded a bit different. Perhaps due to the outdoor expanse in the spot of this encounter.

"Perception sometimes rules deceptive to manage," the Beast chided.

Knack remained silent and continued his observation period. The Beast continued verbally.

"Humans, creatures perceive in many different manners, through the senses available to them."

"Available? What do you mean, available?" Knack inquired, as he adjusted both his countenance and stature to mimic a confident and assured of himself appearance. "I am master of the ground upon which my feet stand," Knack then boasted.

"Are you now?" Beast asked using a hint of sarcasm to spice the question.

"Why, yes," Knack stated in a sure tone.

"Just a moment for deeper thought. Did you construct the ground below your boots?" The Beast asked.

"No."

"Did anyone construct it, as far as you be aware?"

"No."

"Great. Allow me to introduce myself."

Knack nodded ascent.

"I am Deacon Bone."

"Nice to meet you. I am Knack . . . ," he stated, then qualified it by saying, "sorry, my first name seems to desire an evasion of this moment."

"No worry. Nice to meet you, again."

"I suppose you find it a bit curious my last name has run and hid from me."

Matter of factly, Deacon Bone answered, "Not in the least. A common happening in these parts. Perhaps the marsh mist has affected you in a negative manner."

Tiny yet audible sounds, gags, and cackles, emanated from the dark crevices of trees and high grass which jiggled and jutted out boundaries on the path's alternate edges.

"Fairies and gnomes, or at least similar to them in appearance and audible sound," Bone offered as enlightenment.

"You surely jest," Knack emphatically stated, trailed by a pop of laughter.

"I believe they wish to see a show," Deacon Bone indicated.

"Show? What kind of show?" Knack spouted, in frustration.

A rustle in the trees provided a light shower of twigs and limbs. Knack covered his head with both hands. No plunks upon him resulted, but when the shower of bark elements subsided, Knack noticed Deacon Bone had already decided his tool of destruction.

"I can wait, the crowd may object after a bit of inactivity," Bone chided, as a grin poked from his hairy jaw.

"Are you joking?" Knack uttered somewhat exasperated in tone.

A swish sound cut through the air, and into Knack's back as he bent over to finger the flexibility of a potential branch weapon. Bone's thrust met the mark in sound and fury. Knack didn't seem disposed to react.

"I thinkest me branch has the staying power of a rotted twig," Bone spouted a protest.

Knack laughed. "Hold on. I think I've found a suitable weapon."

Bone frowned while bent over to inspect the damage to Knack's back.

"I can't seem to stand back into an upright position," Knack remarked, spouting a few ughs into the verbal mix.

Fairies and gnomes whispered chuckles.

"Hold on, honorable Sir, as I put you back, or, ahem, your back together again."

Bone strode a few steps towards Knack, still hunched over, hand outstretched to the ground as his effort to grasp his weapon of choice evaded a grasp.

Bone collected a kidney, then liver which had escaped Knack's back, pushed them back into their rightful anatomical body positions, then said a prayer using an ancient tongue unfamiliar to Knack.

"What is that? Why are you praying?" Knack asked.

"Not praying. Healing words, administering a balm of sorts," Bone responded. "Not much longer."

"Things are much different here than where I am from," Knack said.

"Is it possible things where you are from are not much different at all than from here?" Bone offered.

Knack thought about those words for a bit. Then he listened to his own perspective thoughts. Then he heard sounds musical.

"I do believe we are hearing Praetorius' 'Terpsichore Dances/Vaults', somewhere off in the forest distance," Knack noted orally.

"Perceptions are as reliable as the preceptor's perspective, here."

"We paint our life scenes from our own pallets. Whether the canvas reveals a Munch or Monet, the street corner is pretty much the same."

"Perhaps we should parry with words as our weapons."

Sounds just above whispers objected from the tree line. Other sounds giggle whispered.

"What do these tree sounds mean? Knack asked Bone.

"Gnomes demand physical combat. Fairies prefer verbal swordsmanship," Bone advised, then suggested, "perhaps we should dance."

"Dance? We are same sex," Knack blurted, yet a bit of squeamishness could be detected in facial expression.

"Are we? Does it matter?" Bone responded, as dare in tone.

"Perhaps with the fairies and gnomes joining in the circle?" Knack posed as possibility.

"Ah, the musical tones of Delibes, 'Coppelia/Slow Waltz And Final Gallop', I believe resonates from the circle edge," Bone intoned.

"Who honors us with their musical splendor?" Knack inquired, respectfully.

"Goblins, of course. They are fine musicians, at least, of the leprechaun ethnicity," Beast Bone said.

The fairies bore faces that looked more like grotesque lemon-shaped masks from ear to ear, and wore crooked cone-shaped hats, of fine cloth it seemed, as the available light of this partial moon night glistened against and in the stitching threads.

Knack noticed the fairies odd smiles that bordered on the shape of scowls, but not quite, and their looks gave him a quiver. Beast Deacon Bone apparently noticed the uncomfortable moments betrayed by Knack, so he offered words of comfort.

"Don't worry. The fairies can't help their physical appearance beamed towards our gaze. They are beautiful amongst themselves if beauty is important at all in cultural matters. The senses can lie, either of masks or tasks or explanations of either or both."

"I've lost some of your thought, but I appreciate your effort," Knack said. Perhaps dance was a good idea. He yearned for one desperately. The call was put out into his psyche, which would not abandon it.. "Let us try for a touch of moment's beauty."

The fairies gleefully expanded the circle diameter in their numbers. The gnomes glee in evidence existed too, but deep within soul, and birthed upon the scene from where creatures were usually hidden or obstructed from view in this type of environment. They made their way, in each group, emerged from folds unseen in the flora and fauna towards the circle shape and completed it.

In the eventual whirr and blitz of sound and scuffle, a gnome somehow managed to become caught between their crotch areas.

"I believe we've been gnomed," Bone said. "The music is so entrancing they sometimes inadvertently entrance themselves, at least the younger ones."

A bit of tingle tapped Mister's loin keys. He tried to ignore it with a guttural gesture sound. "Pardon my loins, sir."

"No worries. Happens to the best of us," Bone said, accompanied by a pleasant and not untoward smirk.

Whether the gnome was gendered male or female didn't matter. The part of the dance involving separation of bodies occurred, and the gnome slid downward gracefully towards ground, and into the wood on and along a wobble pace and course. Apparently, the swish and swoon of pale beer imbibed, at least from the sway of sound in the circled edge of bushes and shrubs, alive with humors, Knack surmised.

Before they re-encountered their loin areas together, a fairy, no, two fairies entered the space in their own coiled embrace.

"I believe we've discovered a new type of dance art," Bone said.

Knack's mind asked himself, "Where the hell did that come from?" by which he meant, that moment or moments unexpected yet not defeatist in emotional tone. Audible conversation continued, but he became unaware of his words spoken as they flowed as drowned out by random thoughts, pumped out by visual and audible stimulations of the moments made here, and curiously towards the moments potentially to ensue. A banter of auditory beats exuded, as if to keep time with the musical sounds' magic.

"Oh, well."

"Yes."

"Further rumination pending."

"Yes."

"Never done is half the fun."

"For some it is a burden."

"Not as burdensome as boredom."

"Yes. The origin of all madness. The starting point and ending point."

The musical tones and notes taunted further, then interceded upon their orally lipped syllable sounds, played by unknown as yet wood creatures, perhaps shy gnomes, and fairies. The forest sounds somewhat subsided in tone, as if to allow for verbal expression of pressing thoughts. Each of them, Bone and Knack, had become intoxicated by the aroma's of the forest, the creatures, the goblin brew they could see and hear swish from earthen clay mugs. Their conversation continuance exhibited a mutual tipsiness.

"A dildo for your thoughts."

"Let's see. I must consult Dildo Daggins. He would know."

"Such course may be forbidden, forgotten."

As if in sync, the forest music evolved into Bizet, "Carmen, Suite No. 1/Sequidille", on cue to their thought processes and decelerated physical efforts.

"Let the doppelgangers bang their drums."

"What avenue of deepest falls have we now trespassed upon?"

"Creatures who emulate us, or each other, not necessarily in appearance. Perhaps more so in other mannerisms unseen to the sense of sight yet bored into one or more of the other existence senses."

"You remind me of a theory I've developed about long-term effects of cognitive learning."

"Oh yes, let's discuss."

"Well, you know how we learn, before we are taught, I call that the pre-cognitive learning stage. The time when we are alerted by our senses of our surroundings, from as far out as our vision can take us, which isn't extremely far, and inward towards our mind processing, the effect when we seem to be able to hear our mind thinking, like a conveyor belt sound, or hammer striking a nail, or jackhammer pounding into a city street of asphalt or concrete."

"Interesting."

"Yes, then we begin to realize there are connections to our senses. They act like nets, to capture what is possible for the physical traits born to us. We then morph into a second stage I call cognitive."

"Okay."

"We process our senses data and try to attach it to what we have learned from personal experience. Eventually that self-learned knowledge it changed by knowledge injected from outside sources, like a parent's voice, water pouring hard from a faucet, birds singing and chirping, dogs barking, cats scratching their nails upon furniture, and the like."

"Ah, yes, I believe I see it, feel it, sense it all now. Just like gnome wine," Bone noted, "an enema mind clean, it is."

"I so need that," Knack said.

"So, humans, and perhaps all creatures, interact with their surroundings in this way, by this means, until they reach an experience level where much knowledge is stored away, but not all needed to be used at one time. But processing of the data in varied situations can become faulty, like driving a car with a near-flat tire, the vehicle drifts towards the direction of the flat tire."

"Yes," Knack said. "Much like that."

"What we learn is we have to second-guess, look twice, before acting on thoughts, if time permits, or instinct doesn't intercede due to exterior circumstances and surroundings, or our fears, triggered, blind us to one or more of our senses needed to process data."

"Examples?"

"We confuse two or more data patches together, not intentionally, and for a second, or maybe minutes, we become taken on a strange path, I call strange because it is one we have mentally traveled before, but the connection in our mind processes causes a confused conclusion. Such as, we hear a name, connect it to a person we knew once by that name, and we start seeing what we encounter from the senses context of that name we knew, and based upon experiences encountered with the named person."

Their thoughts intertwined like unwanted ivy run amuck upon the skin. They began to spout words, as if drips from a leaky roof's edge gutter just after a spring rain proceeded in a rhythm.

"dagwood. woodchip. chippendale. bonehead. headlong. long gone. gone but not forgotten. forgotten not lost. lost and found. found wanting. wanting more. more or less. Poe's Lenore."

"Whether a wench kept her promise, seems on your mind, or at least such a thought dances on the vines nearby," Bone said.

"What?"

"Promises made, promises kept. A noble moral tune."

"Quite impossible, I'd say, in various moral degrees."

"Morale is busted in failures. Deeds of varied indiscretions don't subside in pain. Only in scabs, while healing, are they masked."

"No healing is complete."

"No joy is complete."

"We are all Stoker's unsatiated Dracula, cursed to want, then want more, then still more."

"Satiation of thirst never runs dry."

"The curled worm rests at the bottom of the tequila bottle."

"Unawares of what's about to happen."

"Perhaps sleep is the remedy."

"Perhaps, but then dreams sail the curse along the horizon, seeking a moment to take advantage of favorable winds."

"Drips from the instant coffee pot tempt audible unsatiable taste buds."

"One can only stem the tide, not embrace it, then control it."

"Like the Egyptians? Or the Dutch?"

"We are prisoners of this water world."

"Or the saved passengers of the crashed tide."

Dvorak's "Legend No. 3" invaded Knack's mind space, then slowly faded out in sound while his mind slowly turned to black.

The next morning arrived too soon, unbeknownst to Knack by what means and manner in manipulation. He couldn't recall how he had arrived in his bed. All that remained on the bedspread, disheveled, and stained as it was, were a half-opened cantaloupe, several very wet face cloth rags, and the faint essence of marigolds tinged by a scent of honeysuckle.

"Ow. That was some kind of wicked ale, although not in the drinking, at the time," Knack winced out loud to himself, as he struggled to raise his arms to his forehead, and during the raising process, yearned deeply to massage each side before the fingers of each hand had achieved a touch of temple skin.

His body lay as a pile of stale dumped trash amidst shards of cheap thrill. Cheap in mind, rich in spirit. Feelings of sadness had yet to cloak his heart, but he knew like clockwork, they would eventually claim residence in his chest. He quizzed his mind in self-conversation effort as means to bring himself around to a clearer realization of current moment.

From a face gaze unknown to him, blurred as if by too much light and seasoned by a dank smell, odd sounds of metal instruments working in abandon rhythm, and voices of ignorance towards him in unknown proportions, crashed and bashed together in his mind. He tried to squint a view more perfect but failed in the effort.

"No one needed to know those things, so why would I talk about them?"

"Because you needed to re-know those things."

"Reno. Horrible experience."

"Sometimes the place is the experience, and sometimes the experience is the place."

"Our base instincts are not much different than that of the animal world creatures."

"Fight, flight, ignore until surrounded by the inevitable, then attempt communication, negotiate parameters of thought, space, safety, comfort."

"That last one seems an obsession for humans."

"Yes. Because the others have become mastered, to varied degrees."

"Amidst all of these concerns is imbedded one over-arching need."

"Go on."

"Sex."

"Pray tell why."

"For survival of the species."

"What species?"

"Finally, you understand, even if accidentally."

A familiar voice in his memory then resonated for him a more familiar zone, a zone of latent comfort. Flatus duel, between Beast Bone and he commenced.

Each expelled impolitely scented flatus in the direction of the other, different sounds, smells. to win, each must guess the origin of the flatus, from food consumed, like in a wine tasting duel.

"I once came across an auto accident crash aftermath. I helped remove one of the soon to be deceased passengers from a Tesla. An EM Tech was in the group of people who stopped to render assistance. It was apparent he was on his lunch break, as some fresh ketchup goo drips stained his light blue shirt. The soon to be deceased expressed a last wish. "Mint, mint."

The EM Tech blurted out, "Anyone have any mints? He wants a mint."

Varied hands were thrusted forward, ringed of candied pellets encased in plastic box cases, clicked a last halleluiah cacophony of sounds. The precious mint extracted and plopped into the EM Tech's hand unbusied by death preparation moments. He grasped it between index finger and thumb and awaited instructions from the soon to be dead man's tongue, but none were forthcoming. Only the dead man's hand, index finger stretched long and pointed as is laid in rest upon a dead man's chest, upward, towards the EM Tech's mouth.

A light and somewhat muffled chuckle emanated from the crowd.

"The crowd?"

"Yes, the crowd of onlookers. Solemn witnesses to the old man's last moments. Ears cupped by the curious crowd, awaiting that last mortal sound, final tidbit of wisdom offered to the world."

"It was you. You who chuckled."

After an uncomfortable moment or two, he admitted.

"Yes."

"But, but why?"

"The old man's actions, although noble in spirit, reminded me of an off, off, off New York City Broadway theater program I had attended. A sort of cross between Shakespeare's Othello and Hamlet, only voiced by the actors in tonal pronouncements of politician ranted epaulements puked out at varied self-serving assemblies of slighted citizens."

Try as he did to not allow his mind to escape backwards into the early morn hours of his woodland creatures adventure, and still as yet unknown ghostly apparition characters, ensconced he became in fantasy flight by the sounds and scents of those gathered around to spectate along the edges of the clearing. He looked down upon himself captured in the clearing. "Adiemus", by Karl Jenkins tunefully enveloped his mind like the circle of creatures. At the end of the event, there arose cheering sounds and clapping from the forest folk, but near the end of it, a female voice interceded. The voice of Miska Moonshaw, night maiden, somehow raised in connection her distant memory.

"Whomsoever rules imagination rules the world," the night maiden warned. But the warning wasn't posted, on yellow signs, utilizing bleated loud exclamation points. It signaled as smoke of a burning cedar odor into the airy treetop environs. Even listeners eventually heard nothing, heeded nothing, learned nothing from the siren song syllabic alliteration. Only the cedar aroma lingered.

Mushroom Wars

A sound pounded towards the house, and vibrations followed, as if the wind smacked the side of the dwelling. The vibration disturbed him a bit. The sound he thought might just be a rotted tree branch dislodging from its tree trunk mooring.

He walked over to the large window, rolled up the shade, and noticed tiny sparks marking the tree line about 100 yards away. Another group of sparks skittered across the ground, along and in the high grass. He wondered perhaps if an old power line had dislodged due to the wind, remained active, and spurted out the sparks, perhaps striking a small animal, as the high grass moved in odd shapes and different directions. He didn't notice during his walk around the grounds much to worry about in that patch of the terrain, but now he rethought his conclusion. He determined to check it out, but first he dragged from the closet a long and thick lined wool interior overcoat designed for weather such as he noted upon the view outwards of the window.

Further crack and crackle sounds emitted from the side of the house exterior; some seemed a little closer as from the front corner of the house nearer the woodlands. He opened the front door, heard the crackle sound again, then guessed that effect seemed an echo against the siding. He continued onward towards the high grass movements while immediately realizing he should have changed his shoes, as slippers still comforted his feet, but not for long. Prickled tiny balls, likely fallen from one of the trees, poked at the slipper soles, caused stress to his toes and the arch of each foot bottom. Closer he trekked as curiosity of the sounds and small orange and red balls continued to arch over the tall grass.

Then startled he became as the tall grass to his right, near the corner of the house wall side and the house rear side, where they meet, emitted sounds of scraping, methodical, in unison.

"What creatures travel so?" he wondered. "Perhaps a pair of foxes?" he speculated. A defense weapon for to arm himself evaded his initial venture plan.

He failed also in his effort to turn on the exterior lights as many of them were burned out, except one at the corner of the house which still provided sight hopes. His good fortune dictated that terrestrial spot as the location of where the next sounds emanated in the form of screeches, like trumpets, but lower in volume. The unknown remained his enemy. The tiny ball flashes and pops still pricked at his eyes and eardrums. Completely perplexed now, he was and remained, as the tree-line movements in the distance at the edge of his grounds seemed to sound out in a type of rhythm, reminiscent to an old town marching band. A sentient purpose seemed the cause, and not a mere accident of nature.

More communication type sounds, as if small creatures speaking to each other. Sounds of sharp barks and mangled grunts, perhaps the vowels and consonants of forest wildlife flowed in rivers from varied portions of the wood. Whatever the form of these creatures, there were many, but none could he yet see, and he still felt a safe distance from their vocal vetting, yet odd to his ears vocal renditions.

Feet sore, eardrums quizzed silly, smells of sulphury essence, and finally a clue of sight revealed itself by the tiny ball lights. White mushrooms stained a bit dark and others a bit orange and red, by the movements of the evening shenanigans stood firm and taught. From mushrooms in size relations to the gnomes, and others in relation to him, and still others that stood large as old oaks in height. He was quite amazed he didn't notice them previously, but large ones displayed undersides grayish and white, not distinguishable from cloud cover to the untrained observer.

The country of red mushrooms and the country of white mushrooms decided a dispute as old as time itself: which entity would control the resources available to each. Instead of an agreement assented to by words, written documents, or subsequent deeds, a war to end all wars in this world took place under a ridgeline of ancient old oaks, and somewhat withered pine trees next to his quaint and humble abode. A human observer, a man named Knack, noticed the impending catastrophe as it played similar to many human events over eons.

Knack remembered one of his male work friends who experienced a similar in nature emotional wrenching and reckoning of spirit. The male friend had accepted a transfer to another work office, a hundred miles from his home. Such a work transfer had become all too familiar for this century of humans. A startling reality revealed itself, however, in the spousal relationship of the male human friend upon his revelation of the transfer to his female human spouse. She determined now was the time for her to end their mutual days together after thirty years of co-habitation. She didn't wish to relocate. The female human desired to see what it would be like to live on her own. She had lived at the home of her mother up to the timing of the words "I do", then thirty years onward in the company of Knack's male friend. Now the female human felt obligated to give herself the rest of her days to explore this life option of being on her own.

The male human was utterly floored by such a proposition. He was suspect of the impending phenomena but never came to terms with the result: the desperate silence of no communication among each, at least desperate from the male friend's perspective. Yet, this phenomenon had played itself out gradually between the two mates over the last several years. Together they raised three daughters who were out and about on their own. Now predictably lay forward the blank slate of mutual time for him and his spouse to adjust to a life singularly together as they had enjoyed in the first few years of the relationship, although now privy to much more knowledge and experience about life and how to pursue it further.

Such a societal union of thirty years was not uncommon, nor was a severance thereof. What is love, and how does it work remained a plague unconquered in the natural course of life's events. "Much like employment," Knack thought. When in doubt, cook an omelet, at the least in the mind. All ingredients for any meal preparations paused on the margins, and the margins remained flexible as scientific theory. Room for error scoured the clean saucepan.

His male friend advised, after the breakup, of ruminations he had engaged himself in, sequestered in the Study where nearly all of his difficult adult life encounters became worked out and in plan completed. The friend advised of a walk adventure he pursued for the purpose of further contemplation about his next life, post marriage. The friend discovered a patch of mushrooms growing in the east area woods near the condominium he had moved into after the work transfer. A small patch of woods it seemed, for what he explored by hand and foot, but large enough for some potential edible succulents. But in the evenings he began to notice stirs in the nearby brush at the boundary of the mowed grounds. He didn't know how the grass remained mowed. It just did. But the wilder area displayed a more than wind driven movement at times.

He returned to his condo and searched for some book references, found an encyclopedia volume he didn't recall ownership of which harbored some scattered hand-written texts, perhaps created by the previous owner or owners of the condo, and took in the knowledge as soon as and best as he could. If his land were to truly become his, he must learn of and lay bare the secrets and mysteries born and bred there, too. And so, his friend began the literary journey, in a comfortable recliner chair, located adjacent to and under the 60-watt light of a standing four-foot-tall table lamp. The room displayed a hexagonal shape abutted by bookcases five feet tall along every wall except the front entrance wall. He wondered what lay behind the walls, as the adjacent rooms displayed standard square and rectangular proportions. He remained completely unaware of the habitational characteristics of neighbors on the other side of the walls, ensconced only in the delicacies of his employment tasks, and the emotional task of divorce. The friend lost about twenty pounds in thirty days on what he called the divorce diet.

Or had his friend been captured and caught in the Mushroom domain, pretty much ignored by humans, where a similar type of severance had been taking place for Knack. Concerned Knack had become about his new situation, a move to another property in retirement from his longtime held occupation, much like a divorce in physical and mental circumstance, and how it mirrored the segregation of emotional attachments, similar in form to his friend's state of affairs.

The red and white mushroom inhabitants, tiny and hardy, lived as separate communities, yet generally, in harmony. Gnomes, they were in one section of the mushroom patch. A hardy and industrious bunch. And right beside them, deeper into the forested areas, resided the goblins in the main, but a small band of the goblin clan had branched out generations ago and staked a claim to the Manor House, now known as Knack's home. They used it for safe keeping of their created and found riches.

Under the house, in deep holes, and inside the walls while the house was under construction, these riches resided as safe, solemn, secure, yet the goblins' mindset was tortured and sparked by a big itch, which was the worry of loss of these items precious more to them than anything ever coveted by any creature who had traversed earth paths, particularly odd since no one on the good earth environment of the land, mainly a swamp bordered by unsure and flimsy land masses connected by artificial and wild plant growth, had become aware of the long ago secreted riches.

Knack even wondered how such secrets had been revealed to himself. "It must have been during my dance with Beast Deacon Bone. How silly of me to have forgotten. Perhaps the goblin ale served a purpose beyond imbibement." The goblins' stares and squints during the circle dance, rather disturbing to Knack at the time, now seemed harbingers of warning. Some things must be left alone. Answers not required of all questions. All rugs need not be lifted and swept of underlaid dust particles.

Of common cause and reason, the gnome and goblin kingdoms considered artificial growth an enigma, unless they themselves had instituted the process for their own needs of food source access and community protection measures. The growth of land modification artificial, if it had been planted by human or creature hands or paws, could be considered questionable of noble purpose. If by paws, likely accidental, as passengers on creature back or underbellies. By humans, intended mechanisms created to allow foot or vehicle travel, at appropriate and necessarily efficient locations served purpose, but also served as trespass.

Time savings ruled the humans. Patience evaded their vision. Yet, goblins and gnomes cradled the time on their side, as humble allies, since their lifespan far exceeded, at least to this point in history, that of humans and all other creatures, except those be-spelled of witch-born talents. Miska Moonshaw remained their greatest threat. Knack remained skeptical of his ability to make all of these mental connections in such little time. It seemed as if someone lit or sparked these ideas into his head. Gnome, or goblin, or witch magic, perhaps, had intersected his mental synapsis, begun a work of thoughts chaotic and calamitous, as means to keep him away from places unwanted of trespass.

The Orcs of Tolkien lore were merely orchestral distractions compared to the bloody serenades of the Mushroom Wars. The gnome clans screeched high-pitched daggers of sound able to temporarily paralyze their target opponents. The sounds echoed through the swamps and forested areas like a sound tidal wave roar. Goblins or other creatures standing close enough would become knocked off their pins and became disoriented. The perfect opportunity for wholesale slaughter then transpired, as the legions of gnomes, birthed as twins, an elegant economy for survival purpose, would then drown the goblins, of lesser numbers due to much longer post conception incubation intervals. What the gnomes lacked in physical stature they made up for with superior numbers in multiples.

Cannibalism was practiced by both sides but only against the other, which they moralized as necessary for continued existence. They were too busy fighting against each other to figure out if they had united they could squirrel the skunks (confuse them) and take over a significant portion of the swamp and surrounding forested areas. At this time, their respective leaders determined it time to fight for the spoils of their respective countries. The winning domain would determine domination of the tiny land below the seventy-foot tall pine tree just several yards outside the male human Knack's new domain.

The problem for the Mushroom Kingdom was not unlike the marital predicament of Knack's male human friend. Two Kings long ago attached genetically but now devoid of any kinship union as time had chipped away the loyalties of each family to the other, and thus do battle for the purpose of dividing up the spoils. Upon this battle lay hopes and dreams of citizens of each world, forced to take sides, ignore, or merely hold on during the wild ride of animosity and verbal castigation. Settlement of indiscretions had apparently ceased, for now.

Knack walked back to his abode, locked the front door behind him, alighted the staircase, entered his bedroom, laid the coat upon a chairback, crawled into bed under the covers now cold, and determined to dream of the Mushroom Kingdom in the hopes of recalling the remainder of story told by his male human friend, a long while back, as means to glean some evidence of what was to come from the goblins and gnomes, creatures of habit as they were known to exist. The dream state answered his call. Now, to observe the movie of dreams, he relaxed.

The male human moved into his condo rental on the second floor of a twenty-four-unit building. His unit was just off the edge of the north side of the long building. Just thirty yards north lay the boundary of a large farm. Many tree types bordered the boundary, most immediate in the vicinity were tall pines.

On the first day of the third week, the male human went outside to his car. He opened the driver's door, serenaded by the familiar creak sound of the thirteen years old hinge, sat down in the driver's seat, closed the melodious door, and turned the radio knob to "On". The radio sound on a local news station buzzed along. He clicked on his cell phone and reviewed his email: boring, boring, don't need it, interesting, boring. He stopped reading. He looked around. He gazed at his new environs. He noticed to his right side a tall pine tree just off the edge of the parking lot. A white cement curb marked the boundary between the grass where the pine, rooted about ten feet back and rooted slightly up a hill, towered over the asphalt parking lot surface.

A subtle wind moved pliable branches up, down and sideways as a sparrow fluttered along, about midway up the pine branches. The sparrow finally settled onto one branch, engulfed by long, sharp pine needles. The pine tree had likely been a silent witness to many shenanigans above, inside among its branches, and upon the earthen ground below. The male human had already lit his little cigar and was halfway through smoking it.

The sparrow, all gray and black of it, suddenly swooped down towards the red and white mushroom patch located just below the base of the pine. A rapid beak thrust downward adjacent to a red mushroom on the edge of the mushroom village seemed to satisfy the sparrow's curiosity. The sparrow lifted away and back into the pine needle branches many feet upward. The male human exited his vehicle, went back inside, and prepared for work on the next day. At the end of the next day, the male human returned from work, backed the old car into the parking spot.

Once outside the car he walked over towards the mushroom realms as he lit a little cigar. He noticed flickering light spots all over the mushroom area. The light spots surprised him. The male human had cataract surgery a few years earlier, so he looked sideways at the mushrooms, about seven to ten red and an equal number white, separated by a grass spot, as a means to focus out the glare of the light pole behind him by thirty feet. As the cusp of winter in the east approached upon his new neighborhood, dusk had already come darkly upon the pine at the edge of the parking lot. These light spots raced in a line from the red to white and back almost like fired missiles, he thought. He never witnessed such a thing in his life; however, he never really gave much attention to mushrooms either. Perhaps these were gnats or tiny fireflies he had never seen previous. Maybe the luminosity from the light pole was glaring off the insects.

On day three he arose, stoked more out of curiosity than need, early, about six in the morning. Still, he wondered if this day would become worth the price of admission: muscle aches, joint pain twinges, other and usual annoyances variated by smell, sound, and the usual human hazards encountered by mere existence in the slippers or shoes of the accused self. The male human just couldn't seem to get out of his head what he had seen or thought he had seen among the mushrooms. He wondered if only he became aware of the world he witnessed for the first time in nearly six decades of existence. "Get in your bouncy walk," he reminded self. "Why?" his other voice wondered. "Because" he answered his own self, and for adequate emphasis of cause and course, "because."

He slowly walked down the metal stairs of the condo unit. His hand fumbled in his left pocket to extract a little cigar from the cardboard box, and the lighter. When he approached the first landing of two, he couldn't resist a desire to look out the large window that separated his new home from that of the outside world. He was startled by what he saw, or more distinctly, what he didn't see. The mushrooms were gone, or perhaps he stood too distant to see them.

After a quick step to the lower landing, he pushed open the glass door barrier to the outside world. His heart raced. His head pounded inside. A mental warning drum had sounded. "If I knew you better, I wouldn't have bothered to help," his other voice intoned, to no one but himself. His prejudicial knowledge of a person's pre-disposed wants, needs, and desires disabled an ability to stem his helpful nature in the early course of a relationship encounter. Perhaps this thought process, steamed more by inclination than knowledgeable circumspection, allowed for greater openness towards humans who initially broke the self-defense barriers of emotion. "Not today," a convenient excuse, raised an ugly voice in his head, but awaited presentation of the mood to the listener, or beckoner of assistance. And sometimes, the listener didn't even realize assistance needed attention, thus creating the oddest of circumstances foreshadowed of doom, whether slight in the effort, or catastrophic, and even these circumstances begged regret or forget or ignore signals in him. A stubbornly locked street traffic light, these situations became, too often.

Lit cigar in hand, a puff of smoke escaped his lips. He quickly strolled to the edge of the asphalt paved lot, just outside the mushroom world. The mushrooms were gone. He looked around for dog tracks, deer tracks, human shoe prints, anything to evidence the cause of the tragedy. The mushrooms were all gone. He moved closer, stepped one foot onto the soft earth of the mushroom world, leaned over, and eyed a remnant of a red mushroom but none of the white to his right. He could only wonder if some of the inhabitants survived. If so, the victory had come at a high price, as no remnant of the spoils of war existed. Also gone was ninety percent of the red mushroom realm.

Perhaps the pine tree acted as god of the mushrooms as they needed the pine shade to thrive. Nearby, his cardinal acquaintance chirped temptation to a brown female a few trees over, then alighted upon a thin oak tree branch only yards away and about twenty feet upwards towards the partly cloudy sky which shared only patches of blue on this morning. He greeted the female cardinal in the usual manner, "Hello, misses." She clicked her head sideways and down to acknowledge his presence in voice and demeanor. He responded in the usual manner, "I know we can only become acquaintances, yet I am better for the opportunity as your beauty is a blessing for my heart. I trust your prospective mates will understand, as I have saved them from the clutches of stray cats more than a few times." She nodded down and up, then flew off and away, to allow for our acquaintance to continue on another day, perhaps one of better yielded sunshine.

Perhaps the sparrows were angels working on behalf of the Pine, who had grown weary of the Mushroom Kings' bickering. A cruel and hefty price came due and apparently became marked paid by each kingdom for the disorder organized by the red and white mushroom kings, the male human thought. He hoped, after the impending winter, new mushroom kingdoms would emerge in the shade of the pine, work together, and barter a better fate.

The male human inhaled the flavor of the lit cigar. It was vanilla flavored. He exhaled the smoke from his mouth. He inhaled again. He allowed the gray smoke to escape from his mouth while inhaling it upwards into the facial nostrils. He closed his eyes and felt a slight tingle in his brain. He hoped one day to see the promise of new mushrooms under the pine.

Next Morning

Knack thought of her again, Miska, before even overcoming the warm comfort temptations of his bed mattress, sheets, and covers. He seemed to exist in a vacuum where his body could not feel anything, hear anything, except her voice volume. An entrancement upon his mind, it seemed. He felt the happy and pleasant effects of it in varied parts of his body, over a few days, until he realized the feelings refused to recede, and he became nervous about it. A plague they had become, of his every moment, awake or asleep. He imagined making a doctor's appointment to get checked out, wondered if he had been infected of something.

"Bullshit," his brain shouted to him. "I absolutely, positively do not need bullshit this day!" But bullshit knocked at his front door, none the less, regardless, in jowls of jest. He dutifully responded to the knock sounds, disturbed though that words of rare usage in his vocabulary lexicon had struck like a sneak invasion.

Once arrived at the interior side of his front door, he opened it, at this point devoid of all caution, given his tiresome prior moments encountered in this place. He smelled her scent immediately, then spied the eyes of her face, perceived them as magical as in all of his previous encounters about which he still remained unsure whether those moments were born in reality or mystical dream state, never wavering, to his view, of the same titillating mystery.

"We're out in the country, I surmise," she spoke, as her black gown, capped by a hood, encircled at the neckline by a shawl comfortable in appearance, enticed his mind to explore further her physical traits.

Knack, enchanted still further by her appearance and aroma, stammered forth a blather of words. "We are? How so? By what means? What country?" He looked at his clothes, expecting to see a night robe and long pajamas underneath, but found them to be suit, tie, and black hard-soled shoes. Loss of memory patches stoked fear in his chest cavity. He desperately wanted to grope his pockets for to find a cigar and matches but resisted such a banal temptation in favor of this time moment amidst her presence.

She remained calm, dispassionate in tone, "I mean the terrain. The flora and fauna betray a countrified environment."

Knack had no words, didn't want to call any forth. He solely concentrated to control his facial expression, as mask to hide a temptation to ogle her ephemeral presence uncontrollably. Since he stumbled in the initial word parry, Miska proceeded onward along the conversation trail.

"Really," she said, in a sarcastic tone.

"No," he responded but he couldn't feel his lips move. Now he truly wondered whether she had cast a spell upon him. His mind silently questioned whether veracity of her verbal communication arose to a level of real.

"Real?" she intoned.

"You read my thoughts," he stated.

"No, I anticipated them," she said. Knack didn't look convinced. She feigned a relent to his confused mind state. "Yes, I hear them, and you hear mine."

Knack decided to traverse along the verbal exchange trail she began to blaze. They were now seated in opposing armchairs of the living room, but he couldn't recall the moments between when he opened the front door, and when they seated themselves. No shoe clicks upon the hard-wood floor of the foyer. No scuff sounds across the throw rug of the sitting area. He recalled neither and recorded no information in his brain about these moments.

"A sure sign we are no longer extant in a real existence. I didn't want to admit it. Seems our physical actions are either stunted or unnecessary in this place, as if physicality, except in the least conspicuous manner, isn't accepted as the norm," he said to her, of some tone certainty.

"Well, the gnomes and goblins may disagree, if they cared to partake of our verbal parry, but we and they are subject to the rules of this place," she said.

"We are surely in an existence, just in what such existence remains un-determined," Miska responded in a tone of certainty.

"I notice no one ever makes reference to this place by name," he noted, either in voice or thought he wasn't certain. She remained silent. Illus-trated no emotive response or signal in any single sense of alliteration tendency. She briefly brushed across his eyes a vision of her as a mannequin, for what purpose uncertain to him. To distract himself out of a potential trance state, he spoke again.

"Are we cursed? I've heard you are a witch," he added in attempt to instigate a break of her silence wall.

"No, yes, maybe," she darted back to him as retort.

"I'm no less confused at this moment," Knack said.

"If I cursed you or this place, I do not recall the origin of the action," she said, "and anyway, witches don't debase themselves in such petty deeds, to my mind. They respect the land, and all creatures, and living things which rest and exist upon it."

"That's both good and bad. Certainly not reassuring to my ears or mind," he said.

"People say things because they want to sound like they know something when they themselves remain unsure about what they know and don't know. Witch I am, or was, depending on what state of existence we currently inhabit," she conceded.

"And the maybe?" he verbally wondered.

"We seem to be captured by an unstable dimension paradigm. If I ever mastered significant knowledge or powers, they are much blunted by this place environment. It is a place of both evolving and contracting existence process," she enlightened him.

"The only certainty I've been able to grasp is uncertainty," Knack said.

"Yes. Or non-certainty," she said.

"Even our sensual inclinations act in an extremely muted manner, devoid of time constraints. I'd guess virtually all here exists as a mirage," he said.

"I've already concluded our physical status is significantly muted, or blank," Miska offered as further consideration. "I can persuade the fog to come and go, and I remain able to communicate with the small creatures, but much else is lost to me."

"We may not actually be communicating with each other at this very moment," Knack added, then scratched his chin for a further thought queue.

"Perhaps in intersected dream sequences," she proposed.

Knack then noticed her grammatical iterations seemed to mimic his, which worried him that the voice emitted from her lips and mind remained his own sound merely in a different pitch, such as he might be talking to himself, and only imagined she was there, across from him, blazing beautiful upon his mind, drenching his soul in warm spa waters. He nodded an ascent to her proposition of their status in this place, then provided a longer silence for her to add color into these thought scenes mutually painted upon their minds. Her voice awakened.

"Our one mutual conclusion, I fear. Our current existence, neutral and otherwise, erupts randomly from a dream state existence, and not just for us, but for all present here, including terrain, heavens, and all creatures, and objects in between."

He looked away from her figure to peruse upon the words she had just spooned to him, and to capture some meaning tidbit he could hold onto, if only for a second of time. "The Un and the Non now rules," he thought. He looked down and noticed his shoes remained on his feet, and they touched the floor. When he looked up and upon her visage, no presence of it remained. Even her scent no longer lingered sweet but transformed in his nostrils as dank and dour as the pheromones clung blindly to curious nose hairs. He waited to rub his nose as he trusted some aroma evidence might display a clue. None arrived. He wiped his extended fingers of the right hand across the nasal passage openings of his nose, to tempt an escape of the smell, her smell, or perhaps clothing aroma, or perhaps something he couldn't contemplate and feared knowledge revelation about. "Perhaps it is my own aroma," he wondered.

## Post Parry Nocturne

He recalled an aching tooth on the lower rear left of his jaw line. He could not recall when it last ached. A strange change of events for him, because it ached unexpectedly from time to time, as did his left knee which too had discontinued a torment. He didn't recall sitting down to eat in days, which was entirely outside the normal routine, as the usual appetite ritual required nourishment in some form or capacity only a few hours apart, for his biological system.

Shadows then visited his vision. He heard voices in the shadows. He smelled a fire burning. A blurry vision of alphabet letters began to coax his eyes into a strain of focus. UNREAL REAL. There were other letters, but his vision had faded before their capture. He heaved in the chest area, and a breath sounded out, then he heard a water movement like a rolling brook gurgle. A black curtain drew closed before him. A musical sound tempted his mind, "El Dia Que Me Quievas", by Gardelis, entered the room, then slowly faded from his mind.

Death will make a visit if you want it to enter upon the stage behind the next life moment's curtain, greedy to become drawn back in the unveil of all relevant issues. His mind just wouldn't turn off. He tried to rationalize these moments. "Questions may be answered, or more questions may evolve as answers."

People he used to know yet had not seen for a long while visited his mind. Some had suffered his transgressions, which he came to realize under sudden enlightenment circumstances as flashes of mind stings, yet some of those encountered in his moment arenas had suffered so and he didn't realize it and found out about it later. Postponed bee stings still struck the mark as poignant and curt as any other skin surface breech. A puncture, followed by a bruise, then conceded to treatment protocols as preparation for eventual healing and recovery time.

So too had some benefitted during encounters of his advice moments or learned from observation of his physical actions or voiced words, and he didn't know, but learned about it later. This later time concerned him. In what part of his life did these events occupy his time? In his present state he could not seek out answers at social events. Were the answers hidden in the forest? Did the answers any longer matter?

Something existed in the forest, he knew, because he could hear it, sometimes large in sound but far off in distance, sometimes small in sound but close in nearness. Whether the sounds secreted from the same single creature or multiple creature clans remained uncertain to him, and in the uncertainty an ever piercing and pervasive infection polluted his thought patterns. This place seemed to serve as amphitheater for his thoughts, of varied rumination quality and benefit, perhaps confessional in nature.

Miska Moonshaw Returns

Witch? Vampire? Werewolf? Cratch? Something else? The ultimate life moment had arrived. Revelation. He could delay his response to it no longer. Another creature or being encounter loomed close. He could feel it inside him, the gnaw and nag, and he wasn't prepared to any specific degree of certain defense to it. He had settled into a regular routine, if not regular in the usual sense. A time for culmination of the emotive digressions and aggressions of the mysterious Miss Moonshaw had arrived, and that time refused to leave. Her aroma announced a presence.

Once he realized she was about the grounds, in a place as yet mysterious to his thoughts, the moment placed itself as a ghost in his mind shadows. Around every corner she lurked, near the swamp, on a hard clumped patch of it deeper into the depths of it, behind a thick old oak, eyes set upon him he could feel. Her dank aroma, and his imagination of her dower stare pressed upon his soul to the degree her vision could penetrate his flesh and bone armor.

His amour for her plucked at emotions tucked away deep inside of himself, in a place where no longer could he find even the doorway for entry, and they still moaned lonely, longingly. She sometimes invaded his mind through the screen of his own senses, the sculpted butter placed upon a wedding table as centerpiece for the societal horror about to take place, but his desire never transgressed upon the physical. No titillation of body parts scurvy afflicted him. The disease infected only his mind and eventually, penetrated his soul which had become a handy place to store it given the many and sundry vagaries of life moments yet to become hurdle jumped, tripped upon then over. The memories were so old, the track laid out before him had receded in condition from one of asphalt smooth to cinder stone stained, dusty to the foot touch, and daggered in potential.

He loved her when he didn't know what was love. The spark to a candle and the spark to a firecracker lead to different results, sometimes but not always. This moment of thought transported him to a seminal moment of touch requirement. He rang her doorbell after stretching an arm forward, through the fog shield which blinded him of any sentient physical house perceptions. The doorbell touch echoed no immediate audible reception of his presence. Soon, sounds of verbal fencing crashed an echo inside, somewhere, whether in his head as imaginative stimulation, or inside the house expanses.

Spital sounds and hot blushed faces battered his mind, too reminiscent of his childhood spectatorship of confrontational household adults. Why angry, why nasty words filling the air, he often wondered. No answers revealed themselves, and he wondered whether the answers ever would make an appearance upon the mind's stage. Fist punched and pocked drywall surfaces captured shadows casted by a fading sunlight floating through a back porch window, in which of his previous abodes he could no longer mentally grasp.

His body made movements uncertain to him, but he calculated as ventured upon a mission. He finally realized she was taking him somewhere, but he wasn't ready for a journey, had started and completed many in his younger days, and had no taste for it now. Still, he felt he owed her something, as recompense for her blighted time spent in the presence of him. So, he lifted each boot, although he didn't recall owning any pair of such shoe character, placed them gently then firmly into the muck of ground, scraped against thicket, and brush, and tree trunk, until they reached a dim clearing in the kind of dimness reserved for pre-nightfall ritual. When they started the trek, it was yet to become latest afternoon. He looked upward and realized the treetops were fanned out like kabuki fans, blocking light rays from the sun in all directions, except for the faintest rays that evaded capture.

A small clearing began to take shape ahead, where the sun's rays coagulated into an unusually large expanse of mushroom shape draped upon and across the ground short of green grass and littered by autumn leaf remains, although the autumn time bell had not yet rung. This world of his most recent inhabitance still remained primarily curious to him in vision, aroma, and comfort amenities. To achieve relaxation and the solace of a penance aria he could not find in good conscience, as if his conscience had fled upon his first arrival to the new homestead, although he still felt it lurking in the shadowy places of the house, and the dark woodland areas, tracking him but not ready to become revealed in full countenance, if ever.

A graveyard, it was, this scene upon which he had been led. The little girl of his previous acquaintance now appeared as a little woman, as if painted upon a matchbox for the enticement of purchase at a drugstore or convenience shop, like a novelty item. He noticed no sign of life about her, as if she had turned to stone, yet an outstretched arm ending in a pointed fingertip extended to a direction unfamiliar to him. Many small stones littered randomly the ground, puckered tight by higher grass blades. Some yellow flowers of short stature stood nearby as witness to the imbedded predicament of each stone. He gleaned the purpose had arisen for search or exploration of this area to achieve further edification into his situation, either of the immediate moment, or the many past moments of his mysterious indentured service to the grounds as a whole.

Amidst this grassy sea, he found a cinder block sized thin gray stone bearing his name, but no dates, perhaps because the person of same name as he had become forgotten to the world at large, or perhaps he must serve as guardian or custodian to those yet to have arrived. Knack could still sense Miska nearby, but only in the aroma presence.

"Where are those who have previously arrived?" he wondered.

He then heard a patting sound, as if wrapping paper had been pressed into a fold. The pat sounds continued but origin unknown remained to his mind. He looked back towards the last standing spot of his guide, but she was not there, except for small red blots of an unknown liquid substance laid upon the carpet of moist and dampened dead leaves. His investigative mind concluded blood spatters, but he dismissed the thought as no crime had been committed here, and if so, the blood spatter would have become dried into the ground carpet detritus. Perhaps a squirrel or bird had impaled itself on a broken tree branch tip above, and then drained blood as evidence of a recent in time event.

"Where is she?" he wondered mutually about the little girl, and Miska.

After another splatter sound he realized above him must be the only location. He was a bit too nervous to look upward, but his investigative instinct required a look. He raised his head in order to place his somewhat thick forehead above his eyes' levels. A squint begged need, so he obliged the musculature above and around his brows to achieve a telescopic clear view. He blinked a few times to release liquid nourishment to the eyeballs, which still seemed needed despite the humid atmosphere.

He began to wonder of the nature and purpose of his presence here at the homestead location. His fears of death, and this place marked as the location of his after life, didn't frighten him. Was this stone marked "Knack" his, or another Knack family clan member of origin unknown to him? He had long ago achieved much more than he had come to believe charted as his specific life purpose. Now it seemed purpose in the afterlife beckoned figuration.

He blinked further and further in methodical procession as a means to glean what he was supposed to see in the tree limbs and branches above his head. Then, as if curled up in a ball like a young squirrel, the little girl laid upon a medium thick branch, her pretty dress wrapped amidst her limbs for pillow and blanket comfort, except for the spot just below her neck and above her breast area where the red splotch resided, dry now in texture appearance.

So, he understood. She was his first visitor in this residence of after-death. He must determine her cause of death from the clues found to date, if there were any dates passing as time intervals. "No matter," he concluded. It is good to have something to do in order to pass this time period, for however long it is required to last. Many books, and the possibility of future guest visits, awaited his schedule.

Ghosts of the Forest

"Where is your man?" he asked matter of factly. He was almost afraid to ask. He figured the news would be bad for her, given the state of despair which dropped from her saddened eyes.

"He has gone." That's all she would say.

They eventually entered into a relationship as friends, then entered the cusp of lust. He warned her to not touch the marks on his body. He told her he was so marked, and to touch him was not safe according to his own experience observations. She could not resist, as the temptation to see the marks became so great. He tried to avoid talking about them, but her eyes asked the questions he could not answer. Time continued a grinding passage in their mutual lives until one night, as Jupiter approached the Moon too close but gloriously in the night sky, high each hung, as they clung together, daring the greedy eyes of citizens below. She slowly rubbed his shirt. For a man of 58, his chest was solid, as evidenced by her eyes rolled into the top of their sockets when the fingers of her hands rode across his skin clung taught against muscle tissue.

The man would consult the spirits of this house owned by the other man to determine how to proceed. Eventually he would get around to the ugly task of determination of death, his own, and whether he should be concerned by the possibility, but such a matter didn't seem to take precedence now. Such matters' handling had proved to be his Ulysses' Heel, a moniker he identified for himself as Achilles didn't quite cut it in his mind, to remind of undone tasks he had yet to call forth the stamina to complete. First the woman, then the other man.

How had they together arrived upon this passage of night, traversing the path towards a dawn's early light, he could no longer recall, but a reality of deeds and actions swirled like a sudden squall of emotions, brutal physical transgressions upon body and soul each initiated in passions undiscovered to them either of longing unquenched or perhaps flung by a dullness voided wrench from real, and good, and strong. Howsoever their paths intersected, a reckoning of flesh and bone and miseries past beckoned like the lark's call to action. Tis the time, now, when the flesh of two humans must surrender to a soul's dark temptations, or rot whole in the fiery cinders of regret.

He shook his head violently back and forth in feigned vainglorious efforts to rid the skull of such thought distractions as further sins of mind and soul might require undeserved efforts at contrition. No further need existed in contemplation of repetitive regret over what one could not forget. Done with it. Done with it. Let it go. Let it be.

Then he awoke, the man Knack did, from daydream on a day walk and now returned to his unsolved predicament. "I don't recall such an indiscretion as my dream revealed, but to recall all, at this point, may be too much of an ask," he thought. "Perhaps an indiscretion of others, where I was third party out." Perhaps a guilt trip it was, for Knack, and he himself deserved a knock on the head knot for poor choices. "Other fish to fry," and the imagined smell of fried fish cleansed his nasal passages.

Another thought sparked new mission purpose. "The gnomes must be playing with my mind, to distract me from their prized possessions underground, their gold." He reminded himself, he had no need of it, the gold, in this place.

Beast Deacon Bone was correct when he offered helpful counsel previous. He said, "Strange things happen here in this house, and a purpose flows and follows into the occupation event tide." Bone's words stuck to him like a Red Cross patch. Perhaps not even in the place of his prior existence did he ever covet riches immense, but only enough wealth to progress into the last life moments, to pay for a doctor's medical attention, or nurse's end of life care, and surplus to cover payment to a funeral home to account for a decent burial.

A horrid thought of calculable catastrophic proportions slapped Knack's face wild. "My death expenses were saved in gold coins, hidden away, in a place I can't remember, and even if I could remember, I don't recall in what type of container they might have been hidden, or whether a key required usage to unlock the containment object." And the next thought struck like a dagger deep. "Where did I place, or misplace the key?" He knew night tremors would storm upon him unpredictably now, as his memory continued to recover additional past moments.

An incomplete puzzle his mind had become. To search his books he must, as they harbored his important papers. The one with the least broken and cracked spine was a likely suspect. "Ulysses", by Joyce, his mother's first name. His spirit had finally latched upon a solemn calm. A rest of calm was certainly overdue. The oral archangelic sounds of Caccini's "Ave Maria" soothed him enough to continue along this path's adventure.

Up from the chair to wade through the pin pricks of joint pain, he stood. He moved over to the bookcases of knowledge splendiferous, then deciphered the subject matter crossword puzzle, reached forward to the book frame, pulled from the top binding portion with index and middle finger extended firm, tipped the book towards his concerned countenance, removed book from shelf, returned to chair and planted bottom into seat cushion, from whence all became right and good in his new world. The purple starlings outside the window tapped lightly their approval.

He took comfort in the knowledge he had purpose, useful perhaps, in the afterlife, at the house of Mister Knack. Perhaps he was the new and latest Mister Knack. No matter. To do, and have something to do, served his intellectual and emotional needs quite well. The avian and insect life of his fresh, new domicile seemed to tick along as intended. Mystery became the harmony of his existence, and the tune pleasant hummed along nobly, and swayed a steady comfort reverberation.

"I don't remember wishing for anything when I arrived. And certainly not now."

But then he remembered. While seated in the sales agent's office. He had wished to live here forever until his end days, and beyond, he added jokingly.

Perhaps those beings he met during this introductory part of his new home journey were those he needed to see, to figure things out. His own mind had made the choices. He just hadn't realized it yet, until near the endpoint of this new beginning. Perhaps there were more of them, beings and creatures alike, flora and fauna, too. He would have to ask around of the ones he had already encountered.

Lasting Breaths

A man reflected upon his life, and the times he witnessed a last breath from the humans and animals he'd encountered. This journey could start and end from any possible point or many points. A memory of tasted hot coffee as a warmth from the cup's edge tickled upward the nasal passages yet dispensed it flowed from a brew pot upon which dust had lain soft and solid, meant a distance from one moment to the next had increased much in time length and width.

Just another day in Baltimore. The sun arose in the east, here. Sometimes hard to tell, depending on the season. There existed much beauty, in sights and sounds, and too, much horror. As he was granted another journey, he took the first step, not knowing where it may lead, except for the pre-planned moments and events proceeding therefrom. The pre-planned moments he coveted. Such moments stung brightly in the mind as inspiration sparks popped of maps and plans and plotted courses to known destinations. Pencil notes scribbled; intersection arrows scrawled.

Interjected in the between, moments rare, fraught by frights unimagined in advance, settled upon his shoulders like the wetted flick sounds of bird doo plopped upon a human shoulder perch. Many bird species resided in this city and the surrounding environs, amidst and around. Trees were allowed to continue a service, a purpose, not yet banished completely in favor of the human-made tricks and fixes of concrete, and brick, and asphalt. "In The Bottoms/Barcarolle/Morning", by Dett, waved the human dance forward. Every day's sun measure posed as passion play of merry or mourn, glory or scorn, a bell ringer or mop's plop.

The concrete paved fake paths, amidst faux constructions of habitat, and serviced admirable, if cared for properly, and looked upon appropriately from human eye corners as the time rush only permitted, strained the landscape from natural and ephemeral beauties of many times and many ages ago, as evolved into a worn and near wormless effect for to serve in the preservation militia of mortal contentment. Such need for a crowded, cramped, and odoriferous compartmentalization of human life existed mostly in harmony with sub-species of creatures animal and insect alike.

A battle raged regularly for control, in manners and means as similar to most occupations advanced in measure and course. A battle awaited always near, if not in full bloom, as the roses gave joy, yet the thorns picked at and pricked skins in scorn. Attack and defense and counterattack ruled the lay of the land and all creatures large and small amidst the weather ambiguities either predicted or dared. Ingenuity furthered human advancement. Evolution served a similar creature purpose. At times, a biological invisible virus mutation interrupted the battles and waged a horrid war of its own design. But time kept ticking and tacking sublime.

For all creatures time reigned supreme, as it existed in the great expanse of life and lives, and life itself proceeded and receded as a short blip; a dot on a never-ending blank script of random items feebly elucidated in penciled words, and syllables of words used to construct the longest sentence ever handwritten amidst the trodden and bent grass blades, the kicked sand pebbles, and their cousins the rocks. He checked himself, for to take account of any verbal alliterations produced by his own vocal cords, as his thoughts he didn't want to express verbally, for to reveal true intentions risked rebuke or disturbance of human minds he passed on a walk.

A quick glance around, of eye darts smooth, he demanded of himself. All seemed as it should be, however that might be as result of his thinking, because if he had spoken he supposed some irritation of face like a scowl might be directed his way, but the only scowls on this day seemed reserved for the winds and too puffed and racing clouds overhead as they readied to spit upon the creatures below including him being one of them in the bullseye area of the target.

As was the usual case of abnormal in his new world, he drifted into the place of his current predicament, in the usual manner of means unknown.

" I have a beef with you," said the Beast, Deacon Bone.

"How so?" Knack asked.

"Well, this land, all of it, or rather most of it, used to be mine, to do with as I pleased, and with all creatures on it, also."

"I wasn't apprised of the deed's issue of veracity or prior origin owner," Knack offered as excuse, "and besides, I would further offer to think the gnomes and goblins, and the Witch Miska Moonshaw of the deep fog and marsh, might offer a different perspective."

"Well, that may be so. Yet, it is still mine. Has been in my family for generations."

"Why don't we visit the Courthouse and work it out there. The Clerk can check the records," Knack said.

"Sure, but that would take quite a bit of time," Bone stated firmly.

"What do you propose, in the alternative? Don't you live nearby now. I've seen you in the past and this issue never raised its head between us," Knack said.

"True. I wanted to get to know you, study you, learn your acclimations and inclinations."

"I understand. An effort to communicate." Knack displayed a face reasonable in humor.

"May I ask, what have you discovered about me, from your perspective?" Bone replied.

Knack proceeded to advise Bone of the senses he encountered during the prior meetings with him, then returned to issues of Bone's claim of land. Bone revealed he and family hunted the land, over hunted it, until all animals, and humans disappeared. So, his family starved to death, as they were unable to break through the fog walls.

"I may have to kill, cook, and eat you eventually," Bone advised, "as means to survive."

Knack expressed surprise in facial expression. Unconcerned he seemed, but not too much unconcerned, as he wished to further dissect the origins of Bone's discontentment in their present situation. Such a mental autopsy would become difficult if Bone became physically hostile. Knack parried further in words.

"I have a rare disease. It would be fatal for you to taste my blood, even one drop upon your tongue or splashed upon your eyes, or inhaled into your nostrils, would eventually kill you," Knack advised, calmly.

"Hardly. I am much larger, a cunning hunter. I could stalk and take you down at my leisure when you least expect," Bone warned.

"That you could, but even if you took one bite, or inhaled one scent of my spilled blood, all would be over for you. Your last meal, in effect." He had begun to realize all he needed to perform in order to protect himself was to remove one of his gloves, and touch the skin of the Beast Deacon Bone, and the infection would spread, even if blood weren't drawn of skin or spilled of violent, deep gashes.

"You are bluffing," Bone dared.

"No. I'm not," Knack responded, calmly, almost sorrowfully, as Bone was the only remaining living soul for him to communicate to, encounter, exchange stories, memories, re-grind the past, re-bake into a perfect cake of memory. "Okay," Knack thought, "there's Miss Moonshaw, but her presence is uncertain, uncalculated, and still suspicious to my mind." At least, living as it was known in these territorial parts still seemed a course for Bone and him.

"I know this course and calamity you speak of. I have experienced it previous," Bone responded.

Knack wasn't sure how that could be possible of truth. This land hadn't been owned, except in Trust to the Realty company who took it over when all inhabitants previous had passed. At least, the papers provided to him by the Real Estate Agent revealed such history.

"Do you know who I am, really? Bone asked Knack.

Knack didn't respond yet, became intrigued by one more mystery of the land and inhabitants thereof.

"I am Vidimous Partangien Megalopolis," Bone stated emphatically.

"And your title?" Knack inquired, as a curious brain itch toggled a single hair on his scalp. He thought perhaps it was a ladybug who had just alit on that spot of his head. He was rather adept in the interpretation of names meanings, but these monikers, except Megalopolis, required research to uncover for him meaning.

A foggy haze blocked Knack's vision. Eventually, he experienced the event of a duel, by what means uncertain in battle as objects like rocks, and long strong broken off tree branches took flight amidst the woods. Knack believed Beast Bone as dead or had died of wounds after crawling off. Knack's memory remained fuzzy on this point, perhaps due to a head blow. He hoped he had not touched Beast Bone, for to touch skin on skin likely meant he would never encounter Bone in this place again, and he desired not such a conclusion.

Upon arrival of the next afternoon, after over-sleeping of exhaustion from the previous night's fight, still rather exhausted of his wounds and energy spent and not yet recouped even upon awakening, he stepped carefully down the stairs, spread open the living room curtains and looked out the bay window, only to see a movement in the distant brush at the edge of what used to be the Mushroom Kingdom entrance. Movements of the environs about the entrance, such as birds erratically alighting, small creatures rushing about from the forest edges as if frightened, woke him into a more sentient status.

He retreated from these visions, seated himself in the cushioned chair nearby, unready for further drama of the lands, and browsed about his mind thoughts until one provided sparks, of titillation, likely due to the cold air in the room, but titillation none the less.

"Come here wench," he spouted to the room air. He heard the clicks of her heels onto the hardwood floor, each sound titillating his nether parts. Still flat on his back, ensconced in the comforts of his bed linens, warm, moist cloaks of his anatomy and biology honored of chemical exudes, he reached his right arm out, hand erect, fingers extended to await the presence of her clothed flesh. It arrived, her body, which his vision became glued upon from the waist down to the floor in rapid vertical scans until his eyes became glued to the round nature of her buttocks ensconced in blue jeans worn. It had been a while for him, the time space between these moments. A long time from never, still, passed like not a long time at all. The present moment, conceived, could be characterized as all of time compressed together, in reality. No moment could conspire to pass as anything except past, present, and future pressed into one meat patty. "Burger for Einstein, ready!"

"Backwards towards me, turn that body around. She responded, physically, obedient. His loins rocked another margin forward in appropriate and needed measure, tightened the space in his underwear. He reached his left hand down to his crotch to loosen the underpants of his own body for space access. His right hand still probed the space between his fingertips of somewhat long nails distended, then poked the tips at the back of her left thigh, noted the impression in the jeans, probed the tensile strength of the threads as a soft glide sounded out along the surface. Poked them forward to test the musculature, or lack thereof, in the thigh area, then slid each finger extended towards the curve upward like a fingernail moon line at the crest of a plaintive left buttocks. Of good width and thickness, he determined, as his thumb and forefinger prodded and poked and pinched the jeans surface. At the hint of the pinch, she offered an excited inhale of breath sound, noticeable to his ears, as each of her cheeks seemed to flinch, grow taught. His loins pained erect upon her syllabic utterance noise.

He pinched the same spot again, to elicit the utterance noise once more, then pinched a bit more tight, louder sound, then unlocked the pinch and appreciated the silence as his underwear pants became more taught in thread texture. One more and subtly more significant pinch, at the same contact point of the buttocks, and the woman's breath sound evolved into a gag of short volume and blast, a volume his mind subconsciously searched for a means to convey.

He moved his fingers, as one, towards the crease of her buttocks, as the hand indicated need for further exploration. The fingers began to measure the indenture between the buttocks cheeks, as height and width of the measure increased orgasmic potential for him, and apparently for her, as her sounds, muffled, indicated an exquisite murmur of mystery moans of extremely low tones from her lips, as if she were embarrassed to release the sounds into the greater measure of the room space.

"A bit of pageantry, chaos style," there his vision connected into his brain and began a surmise of circumstances involved. This scene in his mind picture scope went blank upon sudden utterance of another sound. A knocking of repetitive tap, an inconvenient truth in the moment, and much too loud for his circumstance. He stood and walked to the bay window, not in the least confused about the knock sound, much like his imagined and now vanished paramour's heel click upon the floor.

It was Beast Deacon Bone, returned, at the front door, or perhaps a similar looking relative of Bone's not yet introduced to him. Knack concentrated his attention on the face, to make out whether the look of it, chin ridge, cheek brims, eye tones revealed the Beast he had become acquainted to in appearance. Bone, or the being who appeared to be Bone, turned and began a walk away from the door. The mannerisms of arm sway and leg extension didn't quite match, at least displayed in this now somewhat distant view. The brownish dot figure, now a bit clearer in separate puzzle parts of body appearance, appendages, portions, cloth adornments, hair fall, facial manners, as the wry smile usually about to spring just wasn't quite there upon first look. A more purposeful look presented itself outward into the vision of creature viewers, the animals, birds, who gained scent advantage for deduction purpose, as the bay window had not been cranked open by Knack to gain a scent clue.

The purpose, of Bone's destination and demeanor remained mystery to Knack, but the forest animals seemed to reflect a slight urgency about the scene periphery. He wondered some about the mysterious purposes of this land upon which he had settled of late. It did seem to change in appearance, however subtle and suspect, yet remain circled from the same start point and expand outward in all directions towards the same boundary, the fog haze. He reached for a cigar, stored long ago in the box drawer of the table next to the easy chair upon which he reseated himself, spine staunchly pressed into the coarse and cushioned backing. A floral pattern scheme brought the sitter a pleasant, relaxed feel during vision darts.

The cigar in hand he then lit by use of a strange lighter which he didn't recall placed in the drawer, but easy to flick open it was, allowed him some calm retreat for a few moments. The slight inhale of the tobacco stick, the more exhaustive exhale, allowed a snaky line of smoke to bore a trail upward, cross a light beam prone to invade the bay window at this time of day. He noticed his right hand which held the cigar stem seemed a bit cleaner in skin texture than yesterday. Odd he thought it was, given the violent skirmish of the evening prior, when coarse twigs, pebbles, and stale ordered dirt clumps had their way with him during his struggle against Beast Bone's violent inclinations and ordinations.

He realized, at his age, more pleased he became to see someone walking away than towards him. Away meant done, mental rest and emotional burners turned off. Towards meant need to hype senses, brain cells for intellectual interaction. The least energy drained moments ruled the day. Visions of the taught snugness of a quiet room tantalized his mind for decades. Now he had one, and to enjoy every moment of it begged his attention now. The capture of final calmness moments which begged sustenance entirely hinged on his skill to deflect mind darts flung his way by life's past and near-present intervening issues.

Problems never resolved. They merely melted away, dried up, transformed into dust. In the pile of soiled laundry memories, a name stuck out like a dirty sock. Miska. He had known a woman named Miska. Such a thought lit his heart a bit. Had he loved her? Was she someone he had met in his long-ago travels, and left unresolved in the acquaintance some promise? He recalled the name floating about the air, evoked by the gnome voices, as if they attacked his ears using the name Miska. The attack worked, as her name banged into his awake psyche off and on. "I must get off this road and find another course, for now."

"Mirror," he wanted to appear, yet none revealed themselves nearby, for opportunity to size up his wounds and recovery options in time and coarse evolution, such as what scars may arise from the previous night's altercations and exhortations. The sounds of heavy footfalls increased in volume, if even slightly. He could time the arrival moment, began to prepare mentally his greeting voice tone, volume, manner. Appropriate words, attuned to the moment, declined yet to reveal themselves. He wanted to hear the sound of their echo against the walls and ceiling in order to guess their effect upon his imminent guest, who still remained a minute or two from his front door, or window, if a bit more violent encounter was intended by demeanor of this imminent guest.

Cloud fall crossed some of the sun's rays, enough to allow a mirror effect to become revealed by the bay window reflection, of himself, seated in the chair. An odd thought infected his mind. "What if I put the light end of the cigar tip near to my right-hand skin?" He wondered if he would feel the emission of heat. If so, then he assumed he would still be alive, and not extant as ghost, or spirit, or in dream-state experiencing these moments of nowism. He wondered further if the Beast had caste upon him a spell of some woodlands sort.

"I could have been pelosied," he thought. "Hoodwinked, to throw me off my game, as distraction from real moments and meanings."

Head-to-Head

"How may I service our time together today," Knack asked Beast Deacon Bone, who had recently arrived, was invited into the Manor House at Knack's consent. Each settled themselves into the environs of the main front room, reclined in cushioned easy chairs, as means to iron wrinkles from respective matters of concern.

"Perhaps words exchanged among us, as barter, can resolve all concerns, as needed," Bone offered.

"Then let us imbibe the verbiage brew," Knack agreed.

"Allow me, as recompense for your family thievery, an opportunity to pleasure myself upon your physical and mental being," Bone orally threw out as first strike.

"For what purpose?"

"As compensation. Half the land, the other half, the pleasures of your body."

"I have never partaken of such pleasures with a male of any species."

"Well, you presume my anatomy to consist of male features. Perhaps it is the hair in places unusual to your wisdom tree. We apparently have plenty of time, and much to explore on this land revised in scope and measure, and so too can we gather, as one, the reigns of our own bodies and spirits and inner minds in moments of deep contemplations triggered if fleshly moments require need."

Knack considered deeply Bone's curt diatribe. Thought about it for a while, the word sounds, failed to detect female tones, but in bears the groans seemed to him indistinguishable as male or female. Knack further spied a view of his guest seated not far from him, in the darker shadow of the window glow. Thoughts dove into places so deep; he began to wonder if they echoed forth into the mind of this tall, muscular, hairy guest of the light blue eyes and large loins packaged area. He began to wonder what those loins looked like. Merely thick pillows upon a bed, hiding an entry between them? Or a rod ready to spring from flaccid to fully erect, arrow straight and just as blunt. Knack blushed. Apparently the Beast Bone noticed. Bone offered a verbal question to nudge forward possible notions.

"Has your measure of my being met the possibility of at least a meal, as taste?" Bone asked.

"Let us test the wine first, I have some," Knack offered.

"Your offer is most welcome. May I also suggest some music, perhaps light classical sounds, so as not to drain our inner energy from the tap of purpose at hand."

"Your suggestions are both appropriate and appreciated, deep in the veins of this human." Knack's response served as appetizer and small temptation of refreshment, as hors d'oeuvres before the main entree.

"I haven't been exactly honest with you," Knack confessed.

"How so?"

"Well, when you told me about your family claims to the land, not all of it, but parts of it, that corner from whence I've also seen you alight forth from, I understood you to be correct."

Beast Bone heaved somewhat, drew in the air from the room, almost to the point of causing him to gasp for lack of clear air. The gasp elicited as somewhat feminine in sound tone. "Ahem, yes, go on," Beast offered as entreaty.

"I realized that your family had lost the claims in civil proceedings, many and many more generations ago," Knack advised, per the documents provided by the Real Estate Agent.

"And?" Beast realized there awaited a qualification to this factual information revelation.

"I realized the case was incorrectly decided, perhaps due to nefarious engaged activity beforehand, on behalf of or at the direction of people who might benefit from the transaction decision."

"Why are you telling me about this revelation which you have harbored from me?"

"Because I wish to make each of us whole again, as it should have been done during the lives of our ancestors."

"Such a revelation is sweet relief to me," Beast Bone intoned.

"I must ask a question, however, before we proceed. Ah, the wine glasses and wine succulence has materialized in our hands. Shall we sip first?"

Contemplation silence resided for a good bit of time, interrupted by sweet wine glass sniffs and sips, as each enjoyed the aroma and intoxicating stimulations of the moment. Then Knack hazarded an explanation about their mutual circumstances.

"I believe the female Real Estate Agent is innocent in this matter. She merely acted on the proceeding of events, that is, my purchase of the Manor House property. As to the curious events which led to your family ancestor's ouster, those happenings had long pre-ceded her birth," he firmly stated.

Long silence, interceded by tiny sips of wine, and somewhat content exhales of mirth continued. Knack looked forward to a continued resolution discussion, negotiation, then return to ruminations of sexual needs, or in a lesser vein, friendship bonds tormenting each, and how they might propose to resolve them. Their voices then meshed in sound and meaning to the point where who said what became less relevant, and only the thoughts in the words mattered.

"Just think it for a while. It will appear. If you really need it."

"Never thought of it that way. Things appeared and I didn't know why."

"There is a binding of realms, a connection, like life and death itself. No one without the other can exist or cease to exist."

"You mean they are connected."

"Yes. Apparently, now, like you and me."

"What about the fairies, the goblins, the squirrels."

"A story I still read and have not reached yet the final chapter."

"People tend to not hear what they don't want to hear."

"Perhaps, everywhere."

"Look at your ears, face, hands, feet. They are not identical on each side of your body."

"Perfection is an anomaly."

"In other words, oddity is the norm."

"Thank you."

"For what, may I ask?"

"Understanding."

Moments of Knack's memory told him, in spurts, he had previously viewed a real estate "For Sale" sign on a recent sales travel trip. The broker's name read printed as "Unreal Property", or was it "Realty", or "Realter", but the "Un" part attacked his vision as handwritten scroll laid next to artfully crafted and printed letters of the alphabet. The two handwritten letters, perhaps interjected by use of a magic marker or spray paint can, teased his mind a bit too much, and so much as to distract the direction of his vision. "A local kid's joke," he thought. A conversation had commenced outside of his mind, in the air about his face. The syllables of words slowly entered his eardrums and vibrated them enough to redirect him back into his immediate prescient status, wherein Beast Bone's voice took over the moment.

"Owned a car once. Quite old it had become, but I maintained it well," Deacon Bone stated proudly.

"On cars now, we are?" Knack wondered aloud, then asked "What kind of car?"

"An old junker. Bought it cheap. Paid for a restoration. Three-Fifty engine."

"I can hear it purring now," Knack imagined would become the words next spewed by Bone.

"A gas guzzler," Bone added.

"Sounds like my car," Knack said.

"It is your car," the good Deacon Bone said. "You told me about it, and I recounted what you had told me in order to reset our conversation table, as you seemed distracted by other matters in your head."

"Oh," Knack said, recovered in tone. "Yes. Good for hauling sales samples around."

"Never owned a car," Deacon Bone advised. "What color?" Bone orally continued in this quest.

"Oh. A whiter shade of pale," Knack piped back, his irritation vaguely suppressed.

Bone seemed a bit confused, but confusion served purpose. It rested upon their brows perhaps as the greater purpose of this place. Then apology interceded.

"Sorry, trying to keep a view. Blinded fools we prefer to proceed," Bone admitted, "to hide the pain of needs."

Now Knack wondered what was up with Bone. First he owned a car, described it, then said he never owned one. Perhaps he had resided in multiple phases of existence, and in this place of their current habitation, the phases intertwined. No mind. Unsure of this place, this location of many laments, Knack himself dreaded the linen-like unfolds at times.

They speculated whether each existed dead, and along the way to a place unknown, they dragged the sparks of their life moments. Thoughts blurted out as sounds and struck swift like darts against the round and hard sponge of a target board. Their commingles of voice tone echoed into a chaos along high walls and ceiling of the room.

"A dark fantasy nests in the cliffs of any bright landscape of reality."

"But which is fantasy, and which is reality?"

The conversation devolved into assessments of their current and shared predicament in an attempt to shave away the stubborn stubble for a satisfactory glance of a clean slate. Evidentiary vocal points roughly interceded.

"My taste for food has waned dramatically."

"In the temptation or the mastication?"

"A bit of both in the general process, as if the senses required of such pleasures, of food and otherwise taste ignitions, hover mysteriously above more prevalent episodes of memories pleasant."

"I understand. My experience exactly."

"Why so, this current existence status, do you think?"

"Why so, this current existence status, do YOU think?"

"I can only speculate, but such speculation, evolved from much introspection, leads to only one conclusion."

"And it is?"

"We are dead."

An exhaustion of uttered thoughts required a resting point, even if it led to the cliff's edge. Silence restored itself temporarily, during such break, as their mutual contemplations played out amidst their own swelled minds.

"Now we wait, for a time uncertain, what it is that will come to define our fate."

Another silence massaged their moments. It landed upon them; one of dread and doom; another of hope and cheer.

"If we are spirits, roosted now amongst other spirits of human and other creature and flora form, at least we have been allowed our own memories as a consolation."

"Yes. To sort out."

"Perhaps the memories can serve as penance or pleasant persuasion."

"Whether we have been trapped or freed hinges somewhat along the connection to life memories."

"I suffer from an inability to connect some memories to my past, almost as if I have ingested another's past experiences, and I must watch them happen on a movie projector," Knack said.

"Is that movie projector the same as a moving picture show?" Bone asked.

"Yes, I suppose," Knack answered.

"Perhaps we must absolve ourselves of past indiscretions before we are placed somewhere else."

"Perhaps, but indiscretions in one time perspective may not calculate to such in another time space."

"We don't seem to know all of the rules of this place."

"Are the rules the same for us as for the gnomes, goblins, fairies, squirrels, avian and plant life, and other creatures as whomever or whatever they may be?"

"Have we been assigned to this new world as a test, to learn the rules, practice and apply the proper etiquette protocols, as the goal?

"A test it may be as measure of worthiness for the next stair step of enlightenment."

"Yes. We are tasked to learn about ourselves, and further, to learn about others; wants, needs, of body and mind and soul."

"Means we didn't pass the test previously, I suppose."

"Or didn't achieve enough above passing grade to become deemed worthy of a further status."

"Or as is the case, sometimes, too many times, the tester determines who passes, whether right or wrong in objective assessment."

"You mean, the usual human course."

"Of course."

"I wonder what category of gods seek this penance from us."

"Category? I'm not sure I understand. There are so many gods as defined by human definition and practice. Do animals pray to gods?"

"Only the humans."

"Good point. And the animals, they don't have gods, at least of which I am aware or previously advised of."

"Perhaps they do. And those gods are more prescient and powerful than the range of ours, the humans."

"Maybe we aren't located in a good place or a bad place, or somewhere in between, but just a place."

"Either they have revealed themselves, these gods, and we have missed their appearance, or we are located in a place where they may never appear."

"Or we've they've shunned us."

"Or they don't exist. At least we are allowed sensory stimulation, dulled in quality and degree as it may be, in this place."

"Fuzzy. Everything here is fuzzy."

"I would call it hazy."

"Foggy."

"Unsettled, like the white shroud lifted over a dead thing, yet not fully descended upon the body skin."

"Animals and other creatures are not adorned in shrouds."

"Air pockets."

"An incomplete tuck, lacking tautness."

"And tartness."

A silence interlude demanded time. Their voice echoes had receded. It didn't matter who said what to whom, or why. The arbiters of their current and future fate, yet to become identified, would decide. Silence required more time. Granted by walls and ceiling which rested, unable to deflect or echo silence.

"We all have our issues of conflict. If enough time progresses, we figure it out, eventually, in the here, now, or some other place." Knack wasn't sure if these words struck the mark in Bone needed to continue the trek towards a destination of mutual understanding, or disagreement, or truce. Humans created their own fictional problems, he realized during the much time he had been granted to contemplate such matters, then humans clubbed each other over the head with the problems. Everybody hurts, sometimes.

"You have struck a nerve," Knack conceded. "My cigar tip gently bleeds. An aroma strums somber."

"If it must," Bone said, yet his countenance illustrated a sense his own words seemed distracted by some other thoughts circling whirlpool-like in his head.

"In order to think differently, we first have to think," Knack added.

"A grueling human process," Bone noted.

"To say the least," Knack said.

"Ever been to a restaurant and ordered something, then became disappointed by the presentation of the meal?" Bone asked.

"Of course."

"For example?" Bone asked further.

"On one occasion, during dinner hour, the time of day we are most tired, after a long day of work and the many beyond many tedious tasks of energy drain associated with such machinations, I requested a small side of relish," Knack expounded upon, matter-of-factly.

"Oh boy."

"Yes. I purposefully said small. Such a qualification was subject to interpretation," Knack noted.

"And imagination," Bone added.

"Yes."

"What happened, during these varied occasions?" Bone asked intently.

"Well, in one place, the relish arrived in a small and flexible plastic cup, about as wide in circumference as the circle I could make by touching my index fingertip to the tip of my thumb."

"Understandable," Bone said.

"On another occasion, the whole bottle, plastic in surface, arrived. The bottle, green in color, was admirably decorated on the outer surface by the signs of marketers and advertisers, but I could not see or smell the contents," Knack said.

"And the bottle size?" Bone asked.

"As large as the palm surface of my hand, once wrapped around it. I first tried to calculate the means to open the bottle, as it was plastic tipped, and the surface partially remained hidden beneath hardened relish detritus."

"Ugh."

"Yes. I declined to use the relish. Prior instances of such a puzzle presentation didn't end well. Sometimes the top was stuck and the last thing I needed in thought was a frustration at the dinner table."

"A pretense of relish, it appears. And the other instances?" Bone asked.

"Similar nuances of annoyance," Knack said.

"And the lesson?" Bone asked.

"Be more specific in communicating one's needs," Knack said.

"Those who hint at needs and then blame others for a lack of understanding are not worth time, or money," Bone said.

Knack responded further.

"I worked as a salesman. Everyone we considered worth time, effort, and money until they weren't, either because of their own accord or actions, or otherwise."

A fresher rumination silence ensued, but mental communications, self-contained and self-served, still filtered into their mutual intellect atmosphere. Bone glanced at Knack. Knack inhaled then puffed out of the cigar as the smoke lifted in a gentle rhythm trance dance. Each of their actions silently communicated, as judged by nuanced countenance movements of jaw, lips, nose, and forehead skin.

Their mutual understanding heightened. Not necessarily as agreement, or even concession, but ensued like growth of a perception seed planted. Their respective minds then began to sprout and intertwine as vines of misfortune moments each had encountered in their life toils, and so posed a new birth, and subsequent flourish of hopeful and taut prospective buds. On one thought they became perched and sat upon in agreement. Apparently, their minds had been matched to assist in determination of the situation's essence.

A common ground of compatibility surfaced amongst their quintessence courtesies. Their thoughts metastasized into words, then sounds spoken, for approval of the walls and ceiling. Specific voice projector identification not required. These moments marked augural signs of the concentrations and concatenations of creatures matched for a purpose as yet speculative. The walls and ceiling would decide, in due time, the merit of morals in their way and woe tales. The speakers began to learn their own minds, through spoken word sounds of audible sensory malefactions, visual cues, aroma taunts, and physical manifestations ricocheted about from head to toe while reposed in the seated position.

"Jealousy is a demon named heartbreak."

"She used to laugh at my joke in a tantalizing fashion."

"Those sounds faded over time only to become replaced by emanated similar sounds and syllables uttered gutturally by her into the direction of ears of the one poisoned by demon heartbreak."

"Her gleeful sounds of reward for the humorous tones of another, stabbed me mercilessly."

Their persona's meshed and mashed and stretched like hot taffy until their spiritual beings had become one, in concert, of similar emotional break and curl of wave, and smash and smoothness towards and leagues long upon a beach front of placid wet sand. Footprints laid there upon became gradually erased, only to be replaced by others, then smoothed again upon the crash point and roll of the next emotion wave.

"I confessed these emotional sins to a pantheon of gods, and pleaded for a rest, a solemn breath in a day of retreat from the heartbreak on-slaught."

"I fear your evident and likely visible distress, to her sight, illustrated a weakness she pounced upon, like the lioness hungry to feed the cubs."

"Yes. Yes, as I became in chaotic panic, the slowest gazelle, marked for slaughter during the hunt."

"Did you seek a means to snuff the flames of this misery, for to allow the cinders a flame out into the icy cold pile of defeated emotion?"

"I became tired with worry, until worry no longer mattered, as a quenched fire's ash no longer mattered."

"And so, I measured the contents of this moment for to learn a means of traverse along the path not as lonely, but merely in peace, alone."

"Wow."

"Alone gradually became a prevalent god of reason."

"Might I mentally retreat from this moment to call suggestion to-wards, invade upon, the scene in a peaceful manner, as means to further your evolution from anxiety to angst."

"Angst could reveal itself as a healthy and helpful destination. Would perhaps allow for the planning of a visit to the place called destination."

"It's likely visions of things you've already seen. That place."

"What?"

"I sensed you were concerned about your dreams and the origin story buried there."

"What? Are you psychic?"

Their voices returned solely to the bodies of their each and own. Bone began first in voice.

"The first day I visited you, I did a walk around the property before knocking on your front of the house door. It had been a long, long time since I had strayed in the direction of this property."

"This property?" Knack asked.

"I heard a noise and some commotion on the south side, looked up, and saw you standing at the window, in what looked like night clothes," Bone revealed.

"Was it me?" Knack asked.

"Yes, I think so," Bone answered, then asked "Who else would it have been?"

"No one, I suppose. I live alone," Knack said.

"Not as much so as you may have been led to believe," Bone said.

Knack demonstrated body motions of irritated appearance, visible to Bone. Then Knack spoke.

"You've ignited inside me an urge to shoot many questions at this curious target created by these words thrusted into my mind."

"This part of the property, your part, belonged to my great, great grandfather until he was compelled to give it up."

"Why?" Bone asked, on the cusp of a demand tone.

"The goblins," Bone stated, in a somber tone.

"So! I wasn't seeing things!" Knack shouted.

Bone didn't seem irritated by this eruption in Knack's voice. Bone attempted a means to temper the storm.

"The goblins and their war with the gnomes created much havoc and harm, many moons ago, in the time of my ancestors," Bone said.

"How did it end?" Knack asked.

"It never ended," Bone responded.

"A long war. Very depressing," Knack said.

Bone provided further enlightenment of the situation. "More than that, my family, before my birth, abandoned this portion of the land due to the carnage and ever-present threat thereof. The wildlife, then the plant life died away. The swamp land increased in size as a result. Many of the corpses of the war ended up in the swamp, to rot away. The land became primarily unoccupied by all except the goblins, gnomes and their kin since."

"But this house remains," Knack noted, then added, "The voices I hear, whispers in late evening, they are not natural. At first they came only upon me in dreams, but now they have become audible in early evening, and on occasion, early morning."

"For this place, the unnatural exists as natural, opposed to what we knew before we were placed here."

"When you begin to hear them a bit clearer, above the cricket din, at late evening, then you will know," Bone said.

"Know?" Knack asked.

"Know that more battles remain to be waged," Bone advised.

"So even in this place, there are legal issues. Geesh. Or do they just carry over at random intervals?" Knack asked.

"Perhaps random. I'm not certain. As best I can tell, we are joined by this land, not otherwise," Bone said.

"If we are beyond our human existence, I would think we are now in a temporary place. Is there a land records office? I was directed here by a Real Estate Agent," Knack said.

"If there is one, I don't know. There are rumors of an office, but it hasn't been found. Most of the inhabitants don't need one, as you can surmise by my telling thus far," Bone said.

"So, you say I am living in the land of your family. Is my property deed invalid?" Knack asked.

"No. Not by the laws of this place. The goblins hold what is below ground, and the extant occupant of above ground acquires, by default, title and rights to use of the above ground spaces and places," Bone said.

"Justice here sounds strange indeed," Knack said.

"No stranger than other places, in my experience," Bone said.

"Mosquitos," Knack said.

"You noticed. We live bordered if not surrounded by swamp land, yet mosquitos are not present in any significant amount," Bone said.

"Almost as if they avoid it, the swamp," Knack said.

"Because they are a prime food source for gnomes. If you see small bright lights in the forest edge at night, you are seeing a gnome mosquito feast in progress," Bone said. "Due to the fog around and above the marsh, it is difficult to see, but there are many spider webs as thick as cloth on the swamp boundary. The gnomes gather the webs regularly."

"There is something else amidst the swamp, isn't there?" Knack asked in a certain manner.

"Such a topic may require some rest first, before we expend some energy to delve into it," Bone said.

"My cigar tip has lost the fire spark, but I can fix that in a snap," Knack said.

"Some wine may help, in this chair," Bone indicated.

Knack stood, walked to the corner of the room where the wine was stored, opened the cabinet at the corner of the wall, picked a bottle he deemed appropriate.

"We need a small table and glasses," Knack stated, but after he turned towards where Bone remained seated in the easy chair, he noticed what was needed had already been provided.

"A mystery it must remain, I suppose," said Bone.

"So noted," Knack agreed, a bit curious, and nervous, but resolution to relight his cigar took precedence as need. He brought the bottle in one hand and the remaining half of his cigar in the other, held outward from the bend of his elbows. The wine bottle lost its cork along the walk, mysteriously. As he reached the table between the chairs, he noticed the glasses already rested there, anxiously waiting to become filled by the red elixir from the bottle.

Knack blinked his eyes as he bent over to pour the wine into each glass, but upon a second blink noticed the process had become completed before he realized a beginning to it. He then heard the pours, as one imagines a sound, and less like an actual sound. His curiosity seemed irrelevant at this point, and his question of the science involved in these physical actions, and the missing realization parts of his motions, darkened from his mind, were futile to question, as they resulted in no negative emotional or taste sensation consequences so far, unlike his dreams which seemed random, stressful, and unrelenting in anxiety. He was glad to not be dreaming, by day or during otherwise time intervals.

"So, up to this point, I greatly appreciate you catching me up on my whys and whereabouts in this place," Knack said.

"Certainly," Bone responded, quaint and satisfied in tone.

"Still, I miss some of my previous comforts," Knack confided.

"Such as," Bone followed, to explore the vein of thought.

"Newspapers," Knack confided.

"Oh, please. Loads of crap, crappily loaded," Bone laughed. Knack laughed. Then Bone added, "No better way to ruin a morning than to mentally imbibe the crisp, hot fictions produced of feeble minds."

"Good one," Knack offered, as compromise. "Morals matter," he said, then cleared his throat. "More recent and closer to home, one thing concerns me a bit," Knack continued.

"The goblins," Bone said.

"The goblins," Knack repeated.

The goblins. Knack wondered why Bone appeared to avoid conversation about them. Was it a curse to discuss them? Could the goblins hear their conversation, and if so, did that circumstance mean they were close by, as in too close for any reasonable comfort?

"You understand my concerns, I trust," Knack stated.

"Earlier, you mentioned an uncertainty about whether you were alone in this place," Bone stated.

"Yes," Knack said.

"Well, the goblins I will recount for you, their story, purpose, but first a more important matter remains," Bone stated.

"The swamp?" Knack guessed aloud.

"Well, yes. There is more to the swamp," Bone said.

"Something, or someone, a life force stronger than gnome or goblin, I fear, else why the fog cover, like a shroud over such mass of land," Knack expressed in oral wonder.

"Yes. The witch, but why is uncertain. There once existed a large community of them, there in that place, not as numerous as gnomes, but more so than goblins," Bone indicated.

"What happened?" Knack asked. His curt surprise over Bone's use of the word "witch" he tried not to let on.

"The males all gradually passed on, then the females. Now remains only one, as if still waiting for something or someone, or some event," Bone stated, then sipped from the wine glass.

Knack noted Bone's sip, then raised the cigar stub to his own mouth, deeply inhaled to the point of a cough, then exhaled the remainder of the gobbled smoke ball. It drifted upwards towards the high ceiling, readied to explode across the surface as an ocean wave clomps upon beach sand.

"Your head feels lighter now. Good, you need to release the tension before I go on," Bone said.

The sounds of Bone's calculated wine sips, and Knack's smooth cigar inhales raised a readiness for much richer conversation avenues.

"You will need to sit down for this one," Bone advised Knack.

"As you can see and know, I'm already seated," Knack stated, then exuded some laugh huffs, having succumbed to a slowly fallen nature under the wine spells.

"I mean your mind. Seat your mind," Bone said.

Knack would have normally worried a bit, about unpleasant issues raised in the next moments, but the cigar and wine arranged a trick upon his mind, eased it into a landing place for new thoughts. A soft landing, he imagined, and not one of screeches and sparks.

"The witch, you say?" Bone asked, in a means of focus more certain.

"Yes. The presence of the witch in the foggy swamp area is uncertain. The why's and wherefores' unknown. But she is there, still," Bone advised. "I thought you might get around to her as an issue. I imagine you have heard odd sounds, experienced strange movement sounds in the house, of varied pitches and tones. Perhaps dreamed about odd circumstances attached to your life experiences," Bone droned on.

"Does the witch have some specific and related connection to the events you've related to me thus far?" Knack asked.

"Essentially, she rules the swamp. But her sole and lone purpose, for some time, seems to be a search for someone, a male, I believe," Bone stated.

"A man?" Knack asked, but not entirely as a question.

"I suppose. I believe all of us here, below and above ground, and in the sky, are connected, serve different purposes," Bone proposed.

"Purposes," Knack repeated.

"A travel station," Bone said.

"Travel to where, and when, I suppose deserves an issue answer," Knack verbally speculated.

"There are many connections, some remote, some too distant to fully comprehend," Bone said.

"A square has four corners; a triangle three; a circle none," Knack responded.

"You're wandering again. Stay with me," Bone advised.

"Another draw of this stogie should do it," Knack said, tacking a laugh note onto the last word syllable.

"We seem to know the correct questions, but the answers crouch low, entrapped in a place unable to escape and connect to us," Bone advised.

"We need to open the chest," Knack said in a wine peppered tone.

"Chest, as in expand?" Bone asked. He tried a deep inhale and then even greater exhale to no discernable effect.

"Lock and key," Knack intoned, a bit dour in sound. "Find the lock, insert the key."

"Only the goblins hold treasure in this place," Bone said.

"Yes, I suppose. But real treasure lays buried in the human emotional connection, at least for humans," Knack noted. "My sales work experience indicates same to me."

"It is more that is needed. For instance, as a farmer, I acquired seed, but love didn't make it grow tall and lean and fruitful of life and sustenance. It was preparation for the seed's resting place, attention to the growth cycle, and care administered along the process of the cycle that created the finished product," Bone explained.

"You explain a cycle of time progression, however, our circumstance is due to a current irrelevance of time extant," Knack said.

"You mean time has not a place here," Bone said.

"Exact, exact, exactly," Knack stammered out as sheep bleats in sound. "There is no use here for time except as means to keep us trapped, if not completely in body effects, but more notably in a mind mesh or net, more significantly."

"We are caught fish, as it were?" Bone queried.

"What?" Knack asked, but his tone had weakened due to many cigar inhales supplemented by wine sips. "We seem to have all the time available in the world. No hurry. No scurry. No heart palpitations. No mind temptations. A bit of freedom, I'd say."

"And that situation is the trap," Bone said.

"Remember when our days were strictly planned. When time was a precious commodity. To misuse those moments created a bevy bad of vibes and consequences all about us," Knack reminisced randomly of voice.

"If I should think in such a way as you, I might think I was dead," Bone said.

The heavy pall of silence pressed upon them. Neither seemed able to grasp even a syllable of their common language in order to prevent continuance of the silence invasion. It rolled in upon them like the swamp and bog fog, as cleanser of achy bones, or drowned of wrathful hopes. Necessary matters of existence had died a slow death laid steady, until a further plot of destinations became known. There remained solemn a no ticket thicket of purchase available as choice.

"And regarding the goblins, the story is short," Bone said. "They won't bother you unless their treasure is disturbed. It is buried under this house, well below ground level. The tunnels are too small for you to transgress or travel in or upon. But sometimes the goblins will come into the house, from out of one of their secret passages, undiscoverable to humans, to make sure their presence is secure, and none of their treasure has become confiscated. You will only notice them from the corners of your eyes, as the creatures are swift of foot, and carry magic in their essence which deflects a direct gaze of a passerby when above ground, to shield human vision of their presence."

Knack dribbled from his nose the sound of a light snore, and a drip of wetness from the corner of his lips leaked into the tiny caverns of his lower jowls. The cigar tip died off into mere flame embers, dark as night now. Whether Knack comprehended or heard Bone's goblin story summary remained uncertain. No matter. The goblins lasted for uncertain time periods in this world, as all others did. Their time would come to move on, eventually, upon the path to the next journey.

A crafty web had been jointly conceived as if in the musical and tapping tune of Gelinek's "Air Des Mysteres D'isis (Mozart)", then proceeded along as the touch of invisible finger plucks on the piano keys. Perhaps, goblin magic at work, towards what purpose specific, yet to be conceived, just as all things and thoughts in this place of fog and shroud and mystery progressed, sometimes as regress. A brief spark of thought intrigued Bone. He put syllable and sound to it, for the house to consider.

"I think, therefore I am, and what I am is existence."

"Yes, yes," Knack stumbled out orally, across the dialogue plain, in a throaty tone, as his voice emanated forth from a dream state experience.

Bone inhaled, exhaled, listened to the sound. "Another night descends upon us. Perhaps the final one."

Reflections and Refractions

Life, and love, tripped along merely yet merrily, if allowed by the participants, as an unfinished business. Bogle bugle boggled burgle. Anyway, he finally displayed as invisible to the outside world, and he couldn't think of a better fate, nor mourn any loss evident in the situation. After all, love only existed in the deep mind of the beholder, yet for some, it serviced merely a punishment of human existence. He would contemplate this renewed thought until he could abort it and rebirth it, and then again determine if it would grow into worthy consideration. If he somehow might forget it, he knew the voice of it would find a way back to his mind one day, where it belonged folded and stored in a thought drawer for further rumination as a worn hat to dissuade a cold air. He longed to be freed from the chains of his thoughts.

"We have much to explore, if not just in our minds, then also in our imaginations."

"Let's drink to that." Their mutual glass clinks sealed the deal.

"Free as a bird, we may be, now, although subject to hazards thereof."

"If we can escape the cages of our ravaging minds."

"Are we squirrels, or gnomes, or goblins, or fairies, or all of these, at varied times?"

"As the great Svengoolie once spouted, 'Every time a bell rings, an Angel gets its meatballs.'"

"Never heard that one before. What kind of meatballs, one wonders."

"Not all the same?"

"Course not. Size, shape, texture, taste, specific ingredients, all are factors."

"Or factions, like the creatures here."

"Infractions of factions, is the added spice dash."

More contemplation required entrance into their sentient presence, as further rumination, and wine begged attention, seasoned by the smart scent of a cigar, for good measure . . . as musical interludes meandered, eased his mind from torments of dream state imaginings.

Chabrier, "Habanera"

Marais, "Les Folies D'espagne"

On the dawning of a new morn, drawn by the light upon a window-pane partly covered in cloth shade, at the start of next day in a place still unfamiliar to him in the manners he was accustomed, a regular heartbeat sounded, a nuanced vagueness of feelings still yet to become defined, not in the least devoid of necessities related to the usual matters of hygiene and a fresh aroma. A gathering seemed to ignite on the edge of the forest in sound and scent, not far from the gnome villages, based on his percep-tions of the hustle bustle natural woods' intemperate echoes. The gob-lins had already opened their shades and curtains abutting barely above ground window-watch boards. Badly hinged they were in construction to the point of the last swing and sway creaks sounded as alarm for all liv-ing creatures of the landscape. An unusual chaos ensued, or at least an urgency, yet marked of plan the ruckus seemed to unfold.

A visual search of the landscape outside his house, from the perch of a second-floor front windowsill he witnessed what only could become un-derstood, in his mind, as the suspected gathering. A travel had begun, and it tempted all inhabitants of the land to join. Legions and legends of the forests obliged to engage in the occasion, of what purpose still undefined, but necessary in purpose all involved seemed to agree, at least based on de-meanor and dress. Footprints, paw prowls, shoe steps, aired and alighted fowls of many and varied varieties.

Many of the creatures and beings he had not yet noticed along his path walks. Such a parade and march of sound stimulated even further an ex-citement and energy unseen by him to this point of his own and recently instituted journey. For whatever purpose, this promenade of life served, simply as mystery it tempted him, to join, to rub the chin surface of his faith as ignition for deeper thoughts. He made his way through the personal service chores, then proceeded down the stairway to the first floor, where perhaps, he thought, a rescue of some sorts had entered upon his property shore.

Outside the front door he went, not bothering to close it, and the thought disturbed him about six steps forward along the walk, which begged a retreat to the front stoop. This surprising lack of daily decorum and proper form he didn't realize could occur, become stirred in him, to him after all of his many years of life. He somewhat fretted deep inside his bosom about whether the rough circle of creatures off in his distant view defined a disturbance or an admiration of some event or expression mystical and magic and better yet, worth of deep contemplation. He desperately wanted to draw from his jacket pocket a long cigar, to light it, and inhale the goodness of nasal scent, and lip taste of a taut spun wrap as spark to further rumination, to relax in him and his inner nature the beasts of doubt concerning the manner of day proceeding before him and all of his senses, now sharply alighted upon the potential unique in quality goal of this quest. Solar's "Fandango" audibly spurred the march dance in his head.

As his well-clothed physical body approached further towards the center area of the scene, he noted the hums and blurred vocal sounds of the creatures. He thought to speak but drew back the urge. He noticed amidst the gathering crowd stood Deacon Bone. He would surely know the cause of such a matter. He tried to spy the presence of Miska Moonshaw without success. The cigar smoke perhaps created too thick a filter for him to breach in the effort to sense her nearness based on aroma.

He surrendered to memory temptation, abruptly stopped his brisk morning walk, armed a matchstick against the Holy Rosary shaped matchbox, struck it at flame ignition point, slowly drew the flame center to the business hot end of the long cigar which he had removed from his pocket so quickly he barely remembered the required motions to remove it intact and unbroken, and still solid in the moorings wraps to display taught in the mission of sensual inhales of tobacco flavor along the shaft of it. His walk proceeded although steadier and more stolid in pace.

He remained near the rear end of the eager pack of life ahead at the circle. As he approached closer to the center point of the large group, a pause in sound arose to drown the emotional sounds voiced by all tempted to the spot. Something had happened and he missed it. Not alarmed or disconcerted he felt, as the usual course of his life had once again risen up and bit him in the moment. Another just missed moment. But the solemn quiet amazed him to a degree that he moved forward still, although he believed it was time to reverse course, as whatever was the event in view to the others and still not yet him, he had missed the aspect most important, so the other moments to come would act as mere footnotes to the story of the event, and he usually only skimmed the footnotes, unless he sought out one, like on a fishing expedition, particularly important to him.

What kept him still close was the next reaction of the group. They began turning around from the center point, their bodies and gaze, and zeroed in on his persona, or so he thought. He was startled in his comfort of the spot as he had stationed himself at this point to appreciate any event of appreciable enjoyment. He looked behind thinking something there must be the object of their creature and being stares, but no one and no thing stood behind him for as far as he could see, smell, or otherwise sense.

Now temptation of the moment directed his attention back to contemplation of the circle and what might be there. He still could not see exact center point of the gathered attentions. The group then began to part in front of him, to allow a walking path directly to the circle center. He stood back as the others had done, still unaware the path stretch created was meant for his shoes to fill and tread upon. To avoid an appearance of fear in his own being visible to the group, he watched as his latest exhale of the cigar smoke lifted skyward, but not quite as before, over top his forehead to disappear.

Now the smoke stream moved towards the circle in a wavy manner, just as a belly-dancer communicates with hands and hips. He stepped back into the new path created by the group and walked forward towards the circle center point. The silence around him pounded and pounded into his forehead, harder and louder. Only these pounds broke the veil of silence all had been drowned into. The shrapnel of random and prior memory thoughts began to rain upon his mind, until a puddle of one emerged.

"Unreal Realtors."

The pounding in his head then started to recede. The meaning of a prior event had revealed itself cleared. He reached the edge of the circle. No object or being blocked his complete view now. He looked around the inner circle, then stepped into it as the curious vision which had drawn the near entire forest group forward still escaped his sight. Then, he saw it. A flower tiny, yet the aroma drew him nearer. The aroma. The aroma. He squinted, then squinted further, then his shoes reached the spot just before the point where the flower stem disappeared into the ground. The height of the flower was no more than up to the knees of a gnome. A tiny, white petal cup shone upon his gaze, as if a single ray of sun had determined this spot needed assistance for deeper visual inspection.

"The flower of life," Deacon Bone advised in tone.

"Beast, are you certain?" Knack asked.

"Yes, quite." Bone replied, certain in tone.

"I sense Ms. Moonshaw has decided not to partake in this beautiful vision," Knack remarked, not quite sad, but a bit disappointed at the ungranted opportunity to make amends, if any were due her, or him.

"I'd ask how such a thought is relevant to this moment, but I fairly believe I already know the answer," Bone said.

"I cannot honestly retort in the negative to such an apposition," Knack said.

"For another day," Deacon Beast Bone replied.

"Unless history has taught us nothing worth a carry beyond the grave. Everybody hurts. Just a matter of finding someone else who wants to hurt together, in a communion of souls." Knack's supplication served as further penance in the moment.

"Agreed," Bone factuated.

"Agreed," Knack said. Still, he hoped in a much-receded desperation, Ms. Moonshaw lurked nearby, perhaps outside of his vision parameters, so that she too could begin a rumination of his true meaning. The wind currents did not betray any air of her essence. Then again, ruminations such as his may have been and remained still irrelevant to her life's purpose. In other words, he may as well not exist in her world. The thought stabbed at him, but not so much as previous. That emotional well he wished to dry up in order for him to plot abandonment of it entirely. The aches were not worth the breaks of heart stone.

Still, even a broken heart, he surmised, indicated life, and such pains reminded of the privileges bestowed in such an existence, even if those gifts were discovered and opened too late. That lonely box in the closet, not opened again for some time, remained still as beautiful and heartfelt in purpose as the initial and immediate moment of discovery, whether past, present, or anticipated future. All of these lifetimes existed, he knew now. He still resisted surrender to an end of physical existence in the entirety of sensory stimulations, but he understood how a dulling of the sensations could prove blessing when necessary. Purcell's "Chacony In G Minor" stabbed at his soul, chipped away at it, scabbed it, scarred it. This day beckoned further inspection of varied intricacies. His mission had just begun.

The rustle of leaf and grass behind him indicated the moment had come and gone. The rustling receded from his hearing area. But his internal vision remained haunted by one face.

After all of his questions and answers and questions unanswered and answers unquestioned, still he needed one briefer search to determine if he deserved to be happy in this moment. He couldn't think of anything specific. The natural day light began to dim, as cloud cover approached.

"A rain approaches," Bone audibly observed.

"Ah, soul cleansing blanket on the way. At last, at last. I'm just, I'm just . . . just . . . waiting. And there is something to be said for the quality of that," Knack offered.

"Yes. The fond portions of life serve purpose," Bone added.

"As do the food portions," Knack jovially intoned.

Knack was finally in the place of neither lost nor found, merely housed in a location where his properly fitted shoes touched the ground, and though he could not much feel the comfort of such a touch in the space between his socked feet and the sole and heel of each polished bright shoe, still, he realized, there was no longer much to do, physically. All that remained was eternal, perhaps, contemplation, and fortunately, he had lived long enough to have gathered a treasure of thoughts to think and place in a secret chest hidden in the back of a dark closet coded and filed away tabbed under the name "Ruminate". Some matters, like his relationship to Miska Moonshaw, remained as unresolved in death as they had been in life, if they ever truly existed in either. No matter, now.

"Now, to find the pond," Deacon Bone verbally exposed as potential for contemplation.

"Oh no," Knack mumbled. Bone's facial expression seemed to indicate a satisfactory inhalation of the mumble.

"The pond. What pond?" Knack wondered. "For what heavenly purpose?" He knew Bone verbally extended such a purposed mind extraction tube as distraction. Knack attempted elimination of the thought before it became a hideous contemplation infection.

A new battle awaited him. He searched for musical sounds to drown out the laborious thoughts now foisted upon his mind. "I breath this air as pegged and prawned by gnomes and goblins," he thought. "Someone or something above the hazy mist clouds must be listening on a purpose, otherwise, why do I remain sentient?"

"Perhaps there is one who hears in this place," Knack spouted, almost as revelation, "apart from those we've come to know."

"And, too, heals," Bone counseled in tone.

"Words," Knack said. "They do less damage in the voice utterance than in the resultant propulsion smack of their meaning acceptance."

"Interpretation is always the final judgment order amidst any conversation battle," Bone reminded.

A tune entered Knack's head. Bone could hear Knack humming it, but Knack seemed unaware of his own plaintive soundings. Haunts of Khachaturian's "Adagio From Spartacus" seemed a good way to finish out any given day's morning labors or otherwise taxing contemplations. Forever more and never again too often clashed, or more like collided, in his mind.

Always something to remember. Never easily recalled. So be it.

The End

------------------------------------

Reader reviews welcomed.
Best regards,
Mike Gutowski

Previous works by this author available on Amazon.com as softcover
book or eBook:

Amazon.com: Mike Gutowski: Books, Biography, Blog, Audiobooks,
Kindle
Cratch
Time for the Dead: Zombies-A Love Story
Ariadne